DEATH AT THE TAVERN

A HIGGINS & HAWKE 1930S COZY HISTORICAL MYSTERY

LEE STRAUSS

---

*W*hen the door of the morgue cracked open, Dr. Haley Higgins hoped it wasn't news of another body. She'd been backlogged with autopsies since the day the chief medical examiner, Dr. Angus Brown, had been struck by a streetcar and died. She had only just finished stitching up the Y incision on the body now lying on the table. The medical examiner's replacement was due today, a Dr. Peter Guthrie, and in her opinion, he couldn't arrive too soon.

"Stand down, my good boy!" The owner of the gruff voice slammed the door on his way in. "Bloody intern thinks I can't find my way around. It's not my first time in America. I know how the savages think."

The doctor was exceptionally tall with long, willowy limbs and pointed elbows and knees. His shoulders fell forward giving the impression that his head, and its mass of white unruly hair, was in the lead, just an inch or two ahead of the rest of him.

He made a turn about the morgue, squinting his eyes as he took in the equipment and supplies. Giving Haley only a cursory glance, he acted as if she merited no more attention or commendation than the mechanics in the room.

Becoming aware of her slackened jaw, Haley snapped her mouth shut. Her mind tried to comprehend the man before her. Why on earth would the hospital administration replace the late medical examiner with a man who was clearly as old as the hills? And worse, Haley recognized the crotchety English gentleman. Years ago back in England, they'd worked on a case together.

Haley wiped her hands on her lab coat before crossing the floor. "Dr. Guthrie?" She reached out a palm. "I'm Dr. Higgins, your assistant."

The man had a modicum of English good manners and returned her salutation. "How do you do?" His bright eyes blinked as he finally took a moment to consider her. "A lady pathologist, eh? Not many in the field. I've only encountered one before."

"Might that have been me?" Haley asked. "We've met previously ."

He worked his lips. "Yes, in Chesterton. I remember you. You're tall for a woman, aren't you?"

Haley held in a smirk. If she had a dollar for every

time someone mentioned her height—that and her occupation—she'd be a rich woman.

"You were friends with the Gold family at Bray Manor," Dr. Guthrie continued.

"That's correct."

"How extraordinary that we should meet again and on this side of the globe."

Haley couldn't have agreed more. "It is."

Dr. Guthrie made a sudden pivot and took quick strides toward the ceramic table situated under a bright lamp in the middle of the room. He nodded his pointy chin to the pale corpse lying there. "Very well, tell me about this poor fellow."

Haley began her recitation. "Male, Caucasian, mid-thirties. Stab wound. Upper thrust with a thin blade puncturing the right lung and left ventricle. He lost too much blood."

"In the wrong place at the wrong time?"

"He's a suspected bootlegger."

"Ah. Sadly, one must not drink on American soil."

Haley concurred. "That's the law of the land at the moment. However, the powers that be must eventually come to the conclusion that it's a fool's errand trying to control the private lives of people in that manner."

The success of rum running and the string of underground clubs and speakeasies were a testament to that.

Dr. Guthrie grunted. "Prohibition is on its last legs, I predict."

Haley had to agree, though they were almost halfway through 1931 and she couldn't see it happening anytime soon.

"It's the only reason I agreed to endure that frightful journey over the Atlantic," Dr. Guthrie continued. "That and my sons' audacity to move to America. The idiots went on to marry American women and now, blast it, I have *American* grandchildren! My wife Eileen must be turning in her grave."

Haley held in a grin.

The morgue telephone rang, and Haley picked up the heavy black-and-gold receiver. It was the police. After a short conversation, she hung up the phone and followed Dr. Guthrie to his office behind a glass wall.

"There's a body at the Bell in Hand on Union Street," Haley said. "Would you like me to accompany you?"

Dr. Guthrie lowered himself into the chair behind his large oak desk, his knees jutting out awkwardly. He flapped long fingers in Haley's direction.

"You go. The weather in this blasted city is too bloody hot for my old bones."

INVESTIGATIVE REPORTER SAMANTHA HAWKE, byline Sam Hawke, is the only dame on the beat at the Boston Daily Record. *She doesn't take no guff from the guys, and they've learned to respect her, even if she's a skirt.*

She's fearless and tough as nails. Her blond locks and red lips get attention, but the smart men keep their distance. Those who don't, learn a thing or two about the lethal side of long fingernails and pointy-toed shoes. Besides, Sam's married, even if she hasn't seen her no-good husband for a year.

Though no one had ever laid eyes on it but her, Samantha had written that autobiography five years ago when she'd braced herself for a confrontation with the editor in chief, Archie August. She'd insisted that he promote her from receptionist to reporter. The editor said he'd admired her nerve. He had given her the women's column, which she'd begrudgingly taken. Though Mr. August didn't know it, she had a young daughter to think about, and had inherited a demanding mother-in-law whom she supported. The women's column offered pay she couldn't scoff at. She'd taped the biography to the back of her notebook to remind her about how far she'd come since the day Seth Rosenbaum had walked out on her.

Hollywood bombshell Marlene Dietrich's eyebrows are all the rage. Get your tweezers out and shape your brows into razor-thin arches. A little pain is worth the glamor, ladies! Women who happen to lack the natural arch pluck the entire brow and pencil them in with the new eyebrow pencils by Maybelline.

Samantha didn't mind writing the columns, even if they were mostly fluff. Fashion and make-up interested her and her only beef was that she couldn't afford to buy those things for herself. The men she shared the room with would be surprised to know that a safety pin held her brassiere together and that the seams of her skirt had needed re-enforcing more than once.

There were times when facing issues particular to a woman, such as the recent celebration of the tenth anniversary of the Nineteenth Amendment—the women's right to vote—that Samantha, being the only female to report on the story, had produced copy that Archie August had whistled at. Whistling was always a good sign with the bloated editor: it meant he liked what he saw. Samantha had taken the opportunity to plead her case that she could report stories of interest to both sexes. Mr. August had puffed hard on his cigar before relenting.

"Okay, I'll let you sniff out stories on your own time, but in the office you have to cover the women's page."

"Deal!"

Since then Samantha Hawke had made some headway for herself in the paper, but what she needed to be recognized as a real journalist was a big lead.

The Boston Daily Record was housed in a three-story stone building located on Water Street. The "pit" on the second floor had rows of desks butting up against one another, each with a black Remington typewriter, a black cradle telephone, stacks of paper, a well-used coffee mug, and an ashtray. Streams of gray smoke pillared upwards, collecting into a mesmerizing haze along the ceiling. The men sat in various positions of contemplation or hunched over their typewriters with inspired enthusiasm.

Johnny Milwaukee sauntered over to Samantha's desk—the only one *without* a telephone. Not exactly Rudolf Valentino, Johnny had a charisma that outshone what he lacked in Hollywood good looks, and was never short a woman when he wanted one. Samantha had made it clear from the beginning that she wasn't available for dating. She couldn't afford to screw up her job with a bad office romance. Johnny took the rejection easily. "I don't swing with married broads anyway."

She still kicked herself for letting him in on that secret, but it had seemed like the only way to stop his unwanted attentions.

"Hey there, Sam," he said with a glint in his eye. "Slow news day?"

"I'm busy," Samantha said, glancing up from her typewriter.

"I mean with real news, not that women's fluff."

"Women read newspapers too and advertisers like that."

"I just finished a piece on Al Capone," he spouted. "Indicted on 5,000 counts of violating prohibition, and perjury. *Five thousand!* Can you imagine?"

Samantha huffed. "Practically everyone is guilty of violating prohibition. They know Capone's guilty of murder, yet they never arrest him for that. Now *that* would be news."

"Take it outside!" The grumpy voice belonged to Freddy Hall, a middle-aged sports reporter with a brood of kids to feed. He wasn't shy to show his disapproval of Samantha's entrance into what used to be a boys' club. He'd groaned to Archie August when he discovered they had promoted Samantha from her position as receptionist. "We're called news*men* for a reason! And when jobs are hard to find, it's a sin to bring a woman into the pit!"

It wasn't uncommon for a man to write the ladies' pages, and the reporter with the least amount of seniority was usually tasked with the job. But Archie August thought the pages would read more authentically to their female readers if written by a woman. He had a lot of advertisers' dollars counting on it.

He refused to give her a byline, though. Fluff work didn't merit one.

Johnny leaned a hip on the edge of Samantha's desk, his arms casually folded over his vest. "How 'bout I make you a deal?"

Samantha raised a brow. "What kind of deal?"

"You bake me some of those *rugelach*," Johnny said, murdering the pronunciation, "and I'll let you tag along the next time my telephone rings."

Samantha eyed her co-worker suspiciously. She'd

only brought the *rugelach*—croissant-like pastries made with flour, butter, sour cream, sugar, and yeast, and filled with pecans and brown sugar—once, on Mr. August's last birthday. They were expensive, even after replacing the pecans with walnuts and cutting back on the brown sugar, and were meant to impress her boss. And though she never claimed to have baked them— she had Bina to thank for that—she'd never bothered to correct the assumption either.

"Won't we, Max?" Johnny said, waving to his quiet counterpart, Max Owen who took photographs for the paper when out in the field. When in the building, he ran memos between departments and performed miscellaneous tasks.

Max blushed as he locked eyes with Samantha and nodded subtly.

Johnny turned up the charm. "Come on, doll face. Don't be a pill."

"Okay," Samantha said slowly. An actual story would be worth a higher grocery bill. "But the lead comes first, then the *rugelach.*"

Johnny pushed away from Samantha's desk as he slapped his hands together. "Terrific! I've been dreaming about those darn pastries ever since the old man's birthday. Seriously, I'd considered becoming a Jew."

Johnny only referred to Archie August as "the old man" when out of the editor's hearing. In the man's presence, Johnny always addressed their boss as

Archie. Samantha couldn't quite bring herself to call him anything but Mr. August.

Samantha tried to regain focus on the piece she was writing, but her gaze landed on her leather messenger bag. She returned her notebook, added a sharp pencil, and confirmed other important items were inside such as a small flashlight, and a tube of red lipstick—nearly a nub—that Sam wore sparingly. Next paycheck she'd have to break down and buy a new tube.

Samantha finished her article, then picked up her camera bag. The film in her black Kodak box camera held images from yesterday's Ladies of Boston fundraiser. The luncheon had taken place in the new and glamorous Hotel Manger, an imposing modern building near the North Station that simply dwarfed everything else around it. Mrs. Warren, a member of Boston's elite, hosted the event and had given her free rein to take photographs. It was in times like that, when confronted by wealth, that Samantha wished she owned a more fashionable wardrobe and a proper camera. She knew she should be thankful that she even owned a camera at all, but she couldn't help but envy the Ensign Cameo used by Max Owen.

She removed the roll of film and carried it out of the pit. The darkroom was down one floor, along with the composing room, and though there was an elevator in service it took longer than using the stairs.

Heads bobbed up as Samantha passed the glass

window of the composing room and she smiled and waved. She hated to interrupt the men who were busy setting up rows and blocks of type—a task that required extreme concentration—but by the pleased looks on their faces when they saw her, it was evident that they didn't mind.

The dark room was a small rectangular, windowless space that took walking through two doors to get to, as a precaution against letting in unwanted light.

When occupied, a Do Not Disturb sign hung from the door, but at this moment the sign was down and Samantha knew it was safe to walk in.

She pulled the cord and the room was washed in red light, the only type of light that wouldn't ruin the photographs as they were being developed. Samantha began the process of subjecting her negatives to the chemical solutions she'd introduced to the trays.

While she waited for them to develop, she took a look at other photographs that were pinned to a couple of wires that stretched across the room. There were shots of political rallies, the construction of a new office building, and Fred's photos of a baseball game at Fenway Park.

Once her photos were ready, she pinned them to the remaining space on the wire. She'd taken some fine shots of Mrs. Warren. The lady would be pleased.

Samantha returned to her desk and wondered what she should work on next. She checked her watch for the time and sighed. Still three hours to go before the end of her shift. The newspaper had a subscription for several ladies' magazines, an expense she'd convinced Mr. August was necessary to her job, and she started thumbing through them for ideas. If nothing else, she could write about Depression-friendly recipes. Independence Day was coming up. She could tie the piece into that—easy celebration meals and how to adjust a winter frock into a pretty summer dress. A common adage is to write what you know, and making the most of one's wardrobe was Samantha's specialty.

She held her fingers over the keyboard and began typing just as Johnny's telephone rang. Samantha stared at him as he answered.

"Ya? Ya? Yep. Thanks." He grinned at Samantha. "Got a lead. Body at the Bell in Hand."

Samantha grabbed her bag.

2

A small crowd had already gathered at the tavern when Haley eased her 1929 DeSoto to the curb. The cream-and-red, square-bodied, flat-roofed sedan had lost its gleam over the past couple of years, but Haley was one of the few women who owned their own vehicle, and she was proud of it. Together with the double chrome fender, large round headlights, and cream-colored wheels with exposed spokes and inflatable tires, Haley thought the car quite handsome. She'd inherited a sum of money when her parents died, her father having been a savvy investor in his time, and she'd learned a thing or two from him. She had invested well and had had the foresight and instinct to get out of the stock market just before it crashed.

The press, with the help of their contacts in the police department, quickly got wind of each new crime, and this one was no different. Men in linen suits and straw hats huddled together with either a notebook or camera in their hands. Haley had to admire their tenacity to wait it out in the stark heat of the sun. She noted a lone female presence among them, pushing her way to the front.

The oldest pub in Boston, the Bell in Hand Tavern was situated where Union Street met the narrower alley of Marshall Street. The unusual architecture of the red-brick, four-story building reminded Haley of a wedge of a tall piece of cake, rounded at the tip where the pub was located. The view head-on created the illusion of a column, but a step to either side, and the wings of the hairpin spanned outward. Today, the windows along Union Street were riddled with bullet holes. Haley grimaced. Another gang shooting.

Two police officers stood at the entrance, preventing members of the public, including the journalists, from stepping inside.

The news hounds were aware that Haley was the assistant medical examiner and when they saw her, they started shouting:

"Dr. Higgins, where's the medical examiner?"

"Is this shooting related to the gang killing that happened last week?"

"What are your thoughts about prohibition?"

Haley kept her chin down and nodded a silent thanks to the officers as they let her inside.

Members of the police—one taking photographs

and filling the room with smoke as the flash powder went off—were gathered around a hatless male figure slumped at one of the tables. Glass splinters from the windows littered the wood floor, glassware along the tall bar had been shattered, and the mirror behind where the waiter stood, looking pale and in shock, was cracked like a spider's web.

Detective Cluney waved at her. "Over here." He stepped aside along with his officers to make way.

"I expected the new guy," he said. "Guthrie, is it?"

"He just arrived today. Sent me alone this time. I hope that's okay."

The detective shrugged. Haley knew he just needed someone to sign off on the death and if it meant a woman doing it, so be it.

Haley set her black medical bag on one of the tables. The victim slouched forward and toward the right, away from the windows. A bright-red circular wound decorated his vest on the upper left side of his chest with a corresponding wound on the back of his shoulder. The body was warm and mobile—rigor mortis had yet to set in—and Haley estimated the shooting had happened within the hour. Detective Cluney was quick to confirm.

"The fellow behind the bar called the police."

Haley glanced toward the bar, pleased that the bartender—or rather "fellow behind the counter" since there was no alcohol on offer—had moved out from behind it. He now sat in one of the chairs, his head lowered towards the gap between his knees. Shock-induced nausea was common.

"Unfortunate citizen," Detective Cluney said, "or a gang attack?"

"Has the fellow behind the bar given his statement?" Haley asked.

Detective Cluney referred to his notebook. "Name's Mike Tobin. Says the victim ordered "tea" and took a seat at this table. Tobin was washing up behind the bar when he heard gunfire. He flattened himself on the floor and didn't see anything until the shots ceased. When he had the gumption to stand, he saw our victim slouched over like this."

"Do you have an identity?"

Detective Cluney turned his thick neck. "Checked his pockets. Nothing on him except a few bills."

Haley glanced around the bare tavern. "Are there any other witnesses?"

"Tobin says it was a slow period. Only this guy in the tea house."

Haley inclined her head. "Was it really tea in his cup?"

Cluney chuckled. They both knew "tea" was a euphemism for whiskey.

"I sniffed the cup myself. Oddly, it smells like actual tea."

Haley hummed. There was no question Tobin had switched the cup before calling the police. Quite likely, all evidence of alcohol on the premises had been removed prior, as well.

Detective Cluney seemed to read her mind. "My officers found nothing illegal in their search of the building so far."

A cursory glance proved that several uniformed officers were making a show of milling about and searching.

Detective Cluney's vest had inched up over a soft belly. He tugged it sharply. "They found bullet shells out on the sidewalk. It's a cut-and-dried case, I'd say. Capone-style execution. Vic must've rubbed a gang boss the wrong way."

Haley almost agreed when her gaze landed on the bullet holes in the window. She counted them, five in total: one aligned with the victim, two before and one after. She collected a magnifying glass from her medical kit and strolled up close and studied each hole.

"Whatcha doin'?" Detective Cluney asked.

"The craters of the four holes on either side of this table are angling inward, but the shards in the crater of the one that killed our victim angle outward."

"Are you saying that you think the bullet that killed this man was shot from inside the Bell in Hand?"

"Yes, Detective," Haley said. "That's what I'm saying." She offered him the magnifying glass. "Come, have a look."

The detective did as requested and took a moment

to examine each hole, coming to the one adjacent to the body a second time.

"Well, I'll be darned."

"You see the difference?"

"I do, Dr. Higgins."

Haley picked up her medical bag. "I'm going to see how Mr. Tobin is feeling. He looks unwell."

Detective Cluney scowled at the young man. "I think I'll have a chat with him too."

Mr. Tobin's freckled face grew crimson as the two of them approached. Haley spoke quickly to get in front of Detective Cluney's inquisition.

"How are you feeling, Mr. Tobin? You've had a shock."

"I'm finding it a bit hard to breathe," Mr. Tobin admitted. "It's not every day you see a bird kick the bucket in front of your eyes."

Detective Cluney's soured expression was pointedly unsympathetic. "Do you own a gun, Mr. Tobin?"

"Wh-what?"

"A firearm?" the detective repeated impatiently. "Do you own one?"

"No. No, I don't."

"Is there a firearm on the premises?"

"No. Look here, whatcha driving at?"

"We believe the bullet that killed our John Doe here was shot from inside the Bell in Hand."

Mr. Tobin was either sincerely surprised or a very good actor. He shook his head adamantly. "No way. I swear I was alone with the guy." His gaze shot to the ceiling. "Wait a minute. I remember hearing something. Could've been a gunshot. I thought it was an automobile backfiring. My Tin Lizzie does it all the time. Embarrassing really," he smiled slyly. "Especially when I have a pretty passenger."

"You're a funny guy," Detective Cluney said. "Up to funny business, I'd say." Detective Cluney bellowed across the room. "Peters! Take Mr. Tobin to the station for a visit."

"What a minute," Mr. Tobin protested. "I didn't do anything!"

Detective Cluney snorted. "Then you ain't got nothin' to worry about."

Haley watched an indignant Mr. Tobin being led out by the elbow to a police car parked on Marshall Street. Just as the door opened, Haley caught sight of the morgue van waiting.

Inside, Detective Cluney consulted with an officer. When Haley approached, he said, "No bullet shells inside, but they collected four from outside."

"Not five?"

The detective confirmed it by a quick shake of his head.

"The killer must've picked it up off the floor," Haley said, now completely convinced the dead man had been shot from inside the tavern.

The detective raised his voice to address one of his men. "Check behind the bar and have a look in Tobin's locker." To Haley, he added, "I asked Peters to check Tobin's pockets. I'll let you know if he finds anything."

Haley exited through the Marshall street door to wave in the driver of the morgue van and supervised as he and a police officer rolled the gurney with the body outside.

As Haley knew he would, Detective Cluney left via Union Street to take on the reporters. He'd swear up and down that he hated that part of his job, but Haley suspected he secretly liked the attention.

Wanting to avoid the news folks, Haley decided to walk around the building, rather than through, even though it would take longer to get to her car. She even went further out of her way to cross Union Street, giving the journalists a wide berth. She'd had plenty of encounters with pushy and insensitive reporters, and did whatever she could to avoid them.

Haley reached her DeSoto, unlocked the door, and was about to slide inside, when a female voice called for her.

"Dr. Higgins!"

Haley was surprised to see the woman reporter she'd spotted earlier and huffed in frustration. Why hadn't she stayed with the others to question Detective Cluney?

"Yes?"

"I'm investigative reporter Sam Hawke, Samantha actually, but you know, it's a man's world."

Haley nodded. This was a truth she and this reporter shared.

"Would you mind if I asked you a few questions?"

Haley considered the woman whose straw hat angled sharply along the right side of her head. Even though the blond at her temple was damp with sweat, and natural spots of red colored creamy cheeks, she remained attractive. Her rayon dress suit fit nicely on a slender, hourglass frame, but it wasn't new. Her expression, close to desperation, flashed behind large eyes. Haley didn't have the heart to turn her away.

"I'm in a hurry, so if you don't mind riding with me. I can drop you off at the paper. Which one is it?"

Miss Hawke jumped into the passenger seat, shuffling her messenger bag inside with her. "*The Daily Record.*"

Haley checked her rearview mirror and signaled before making a U-turn. She shot her unwanted passenger a glance.

"So, Miss Hawke, what would you like to ask me?"

3

*B*eing the lone newswoman at the paper had its advantages, and Samantha wasn't beyond using her feminine charms to get what she wanted. She never felt bad about it. The female gender had very few advantages, even in these modern times. The batting of the eyes, a flirtatious smile, a pronounced wiggle in the hips, an extra inch of exposed leg. Harmless, yet effective. It had gotten her this story. Two stories, actually, but Johnny only knew of this one.

While sitting alone at a window booth, an unidentified man was shot and killed in the Bell in Hand Tavern on Union Street as he drank a cup of tea. Several bullet holes had pierced the windows. According to the lead police officer, Detective Emmet Cluney, the incident was likely gang related, but the situation is still under investigation.

Samantha finished the piece with statistics on gang and Mob-related crime and how it had escalated since prohibition. She rolled the page out of the typewriter's cylinder. Lowering her chin, she stared at Johnny with wide eyes. "I'll deliver this to Mr. August myself if you don't mind."

"I can walk with you."

"No need," Samantha said with gentle laughter. "I know the way."

Aware of the lingering gazes of most of the men in the room, including Johnny and Max, and a sneer from Freddy Hall, she strolled past the framed picture of Abraham Lincoln that hung on the wall and down the hallway to the office of the editor.

Archie August looked up at her over round eyeglasses with a mixed look of surprise and annoyance. A competitor's newspaper was opened on his large oak desk.

"You can put your ladies' piece in my inbox."

"This is the story on the shooting at the Bell in Hand. Johnny thinks we can get it out in the evening press if we hurry."

"*You* wrote it?" he said with the same incredulity as if he suspected a dog had written it. Samantha swallowed her offense. "Yes, sir. Max has the photos hanging in the dark room."

LEE STRAUSS

Mr. August folded his newspaper and pushed it to the side before placing the sheet of paper Samantha had offered on the desk in front of him. He opened a drawer and removed a blue pencil, pushed his glasses up the bridge of his flat nose, and squinted.

"Uh-uh, uh-uh."

Samantha couldn't tell if her boss's grunts were positive or negative.

"Hmmm."

He scribbled all over it with the blue pencil and Samantha nibbled her lip. The fact that her editor was taking time to doodle meant it wasn't a waste of his time. Didn't mean he liked it enough to print it, though.

Mr. August delivered his verdict. "Not bad, Miss Hawke. You can run with it." He handed it back and without another glance at Samantha, opened the *Globe and Mail*.

"Thank you, sir," Samantha said quickly, making her exit before the man could change his mind.

Back in the pit, she worked madly on the corrections and then announced that the piece was good to go. Johnny, now busy with something at his desk, shot Samantha a quick look. "Take it down to Inky, then."

Simeon "Inky" Isaacson managed composing one floor down, and the printing press crew in the basement. Samantha pinched her copy tightly and took the stairs.

Her presence in the composing room brought the

men who worked there to a momentary standstill. Inky, a small, wiry man, clapped his ink-stained hands.

"Get back to work! It's not like you ain't seen a lady before."

With quick, short steps, he hustled to the door where Samantha waited.

"Miss Hawke?" His surprise and amusement were evident on his wrinkled face. "Mr. August needin' somethin'?"

Samantha held out the sheet of paper with her story.

"This needs to make tonight's paper, if possible."

Inky scrunched up his nose as he read. His eyes darted back to Samantha. "The boss approved the byline?"

Samantha swallowed her annoyance. Inky wouldn't have asked about the byline if it hadn't read Sam Hawke.

"I wrote the piece," Samantha said indignantly. "It's my byline."

"Inky's lips pulled into a smile, revealing tobacco-stained teeth. "Very well. We'll get it in tonight's run."

Before Samantha could offer her thanks, Inky was halfway across the room shouting instructions to a group of men huddled around one of the composing tables. She took a moment to watch with wonder as they selected stamps with inverted letters of the alphabet and painstakingly recreated the story for type.

When Samantha returned to her desk, she inserted a fresh piece of paper.

I recently met the intriguing Dr. Haley Higgins, the City of Boston's assistant medical examiner, while on a story about another apparent Mob-related shooting in the North End. Striking in many ways, Dr. Higgins is . . .

Samantha paused and stared at the ceiling as her mind grasped for words. *A thoroughly modern woman.* . .

Inspired, Samantha let her fingers start flying across the keys.

THE MORGUE WAS in the basement of the Mass-achusetts General Hospital which sat on a large corner lot where Allen Street met Charles Street adjacent to the Charles River embankment. The room was painted white and was well lit with large electric lamps. There was a ceramic autopsy table, a wooden table for miscellaneous tasks, and a long counter with test tubes, glass cylinders, Bunsen burners, and other tools used for performing the corresponding tests. A large wooden desk belonging to Haley sat in one corner. Near it was a small table equipped with an electric kettle for tea, and a percolator to make coffee. Haley preferred the glass cylinder French press that she'd ordered from Paris. It was simpler to use than the percolating procedure, quicker, and in her opinion, made a superior brew. Along the far wall were rows of refrigerated cabinets that held the bodies either waiting for autopsies or waiting to be delivered to a neighboring undertaker.

Currently, Haley was assisting Dr. Guthrie with the autopsy of their John Doe from the Bell in Hand. The Y incision revealed the chest cavity. The bullet hole that had penetrated the heart would've killed the victim immediately.

"Detective Cluney believes a Mob gang targeted the man," she said.

Dr. Guthrie grunted. "I don't trust the Irish."

Haley wasn't surprised by the Englishman's words. It was well known that the English and Irish, in Europe and America, weren't exactly on friendly terms. And there were many Bostonians who agreed with that statement. Of course, they were the same ones who didn't trust the Italians or the Jews either.

"Detective Cluney is one of the good ones," Haley said. Unfortunately, there were many officers on the force who were corrupt at one level or another. The Depression was hard on everyone—even an honest cop could be tempted if it meant feeding his family.

"But," she continued, "I'm not sure if I agree with his assessment."

"Why not?"

Haley relayed the difference in the crater direction

of the shot that must've killed the man. "The other shots were just for show."

"I thought you said he was alone in the room."

"That's what the man behind the counter claimed."

"You don't believe him?"

Haley shrugged. "He says he flattened himself to the floor when he heard the first shot. Swears he didn't see a thing."

"About those other shots," Dr. Guthrie said. "Could this man have had so many enemies that two different attempts on his life were taken at the same time?"

Haley conceded. "It is a bit of a stretch."

Dr. Guthrie left Haley to stitch up the Y incision. Out of the corner of her eye, Haley watched him through the glass wall of his office as he lit a pipe, leaned back in his chair with eyes closed, and released a puff of smoke out of the corner of his mouth.

She'd just finished the final stitch when a sharp tap caught her attention. The door to the morgue opened and Detective Cluney's round head popped through the crack.

"Hope I'm not interrupting," he said, completing his journey inside. He strode over to Dr. Guthrie and extended a hand. "Detective Cluney. Welcome to Boston."

Dr. Guthrie was an English gentleman. He stood and accepted the proffered hand, but suspicion flashed behind his eyes. Unlike Chesterton, Boston was filled with non-English folk, and it would likely take a while, if ever, for the doctor to change his biases.

Detective Cluney turned to Haley. "Thought you might like to know that we've identified the vic. Name's Stefano Marchesi."

Haley's dark brows arched. "Of the Marchesi gang?"

"The same. Apparently this fellow's estranged. Tried to distance himself from his Mob family. Even Anglicized his name to Stephen March."

Haley was incredulous. "Do you think his family killed him?"

"Nothin' surprises me these days. I wonder what he did to tip their boat?" The detective rocked on his heels. "The Marchesis don't play nice. I've seen what they do to those who cross them. I can only imagine what they'd do if they felt betrayed by their own flesh and blood."

Haley's curiosity was piqued. She glanced at the body of Stefano Marchesi and wondered what he'd done that was so bad his own family felt he deserved to die.

As Haley suspected, Detective Cluney hadn't dropped in purely out of the goodness of his heart. He wanted something in return.

He nodded toward the body. "You got anything for me?"

Dr. Guthrie grunted. "Cause of death: bullet through the heart. Close proximity."

"How close?" the detective asked.

"Within four feet," Haley said. "Close enough for gunshot residue to collect on the victim's clothing."

"So, you're saying for certain that the bullet that killed him came from inside the tavern and not from a passing car."

"We are."

4

Samantha fanned herself with her gloves as she briskly walked home from the office to her apartment on Stillman Street. The redbrick, flat-faced tenement building was among a row of others like it on the south point of what had once been a vibrant Jewish neighborhood. Just a block or two away was a "hotel" that everyone knew was a brothel, including the police in so much as they turned a blind eye. Like alcohol, prostitution was illegal, but also like alcohol, those who wanted the vice could find it.

Samantha hurried inside. Her mother-in-law Bina and her six-year-old daughter Talia waited inside their second-floor apartment.

A slight, stern-looking lady, hardly five feet tall, Bina Rosenbaum took no guff. The lines on her face and the hunch of her back spoke of a difficult life. With a German-Jewish heritage, she and her late husband had immigrated to Boston in 1919, just after the Great War. Samantha had to stir up her empathy daily to remain civil.

"There you are!" Bina declared as she did every single day. She had a way of making Samantha guilty of something, even if it was going to work so they could eat and stay warm in the winter.

"Yes, here I am." Samantha bent a knee as Talia rushed into her arms.

"Mommy!"

"Hi there, honey."

Talia shared Samantha's honey-blond locks and bright blue eyes. Staring at her daughter was like staring at the rare photograph of herself when she was a child.

Samantha kissed the top of Talia's head. "How was school today?"

Talia grew quiet. "Fine."

"You should send her to a Jewish school," Bina said from behind the kitchen wall. "Those other kids tease her."

"Why?" Samantha said. This was the first she'd heard of any ill-treatment of her daughter.

"*Vilde chaya!*" Bina said. She thought all gentiles were wild animals. "Because she's Jewish, that's why. The Italians are the worst." Bina pointed her wooden spoon. "Did you know that the Brumbergs have moved out of the building now? They've gone to the South End too. Now another Italian family is moving in. We used to attend synagogue together, we were one big family, and now, now, I feel like an orphan. I'm going to die in *Italia!*"

Bina wasn't exaggerating. Many Jewish families had left the North End, feeling unwelcome by the mass of new immigrants. The citizens who claimed Puritan roots, much like Samantha herself, were not much better.

"If only Seth were here," Bina moaned.

When Seth Rosenbaum—Samantha's no-good husband—had left, it forced Samantha to look for work. She knew she wouldn't use his name. Finding a job as a single woman was tough enough, and for married women, it was nearly impossible. And, in these tough times, sounding Jewish would only make it worse. Hawke was Samantha's maiden name, and she was happy to use it.

Besides, if it weren't for Talia, Bina wouldn't even recognize their marriage. Samantha and Seth had tied the knot in a courthouse because she wasn't Jewish (at the age of nineteen and already with child), and Seth didn't want to have to deal with the fuss of a ceremonial marriage.

Even though the quick and easy wedding had been his idea (to make an honest woman of her!), Bina always blamed Samantha for it. *The embarrassment is too much!* Bina had recited this phrase like a mantra. It took her weeks before she'd go out in public and dare to look people in the eye.

To Bina, Samantha said, "Why do you keep bringing him up? And please, not in front of—" She tilted her head toward Talia.

"Because he's my son and her father. You can't keep the truth from her forever."

"What *truth* are you speaking of?" Samantha stormed to her room before her aggravating mother-in-law could answer. They would never agree when it came to Seth. Samantha knew her husband was a thief and a liar, and worse than that, he'd abandoned his family. But to Bina, Seth would always be her dear boy who could do no wrong. She was convinced that her son lay dead in a ditch somewhere. It was the only way she could accept that he was probably gone for good.

And maybe Bina was right. Maybe Seth was dead. It didn't matter to Samantha. He was as good as dead to her anyway.

"Mommy?" Talia slipped silently into the bedroom. It was small with two dressers and a double bed they shared.

"Honey?"

Talia sat on the edge of the bed and clung to the metal footboard. "Why do you and Bubba always fight?"

"We don't always fight."

"Yes, you do."

Samantha put an arm around Talia's slim shoulders. "It might sound like we do, but that's how Bubba and I communicate. It's just her way."

"She's not going to leave us, is she?"

"What? No! Of course not. Why would you think that?"

"Because the Garfields and the Yagers have left. Bubba misses them."

Samantha's heart pinched for her daughter. "Oh, honey. Bubba's not going to leave us. We are family. And sometimes families argue."

"Do you love Bubba?"

"Of course I do." Despite Bina's dominating personality, the woman was the only mother figure Samantha had. Her mother had died of Spanish influenza when Samantha was fourteen.

"Do you love Daddy?"

Oh, dear. The questions from her sweet girl were getting trickier. Samantha sensed there was a deeper question wrapped in that one.

"The love between a man and a woman is very different from the love between a mother and daughter. It's true that my feelings for your father changed over time, but that will never happen with you. Never."

"Will Daddy ever come home?"

"I don't know, honey. I don't know. Now let's go eat. You know how much of a bear Bubba becomes when we're late to the table."

Their home was simple. The kitchen contained a wooden table with four matching chairs. Attached was a modest living room with a divan and two armchairs. The cream-and-green floral-print wallpaper pulled away at the seams and the corners.

Bina had cooked vegetable soup and dumplings. It wasn't much, but enough to fill their empty stomachs.

They ate with little chitchat, and Samantha's mind returned to the events of the day. Finally writing something that didn't end up solely in the ladies' pages. Seeing the scene of the crime, at least the part that could be seen from the street. Meeting Dr. Higgins. Though she hadn't said so in so many words, Samantha got a sense that the forensic pathologist didn't think the shooting was gang related or random. Samantha tended to agree. Her gut told her there was more.

Maybe it was just wishful thinking. Writing a story was one thing, breaking it was another, and the one thing she dreamed of doing was breaking a big story. Then Mr. August would have to treat her like one of the guys. Then he'd have to give her a raise. As it was, she knew she was making a third of what Johnny made, and he was single. She supported a family of three.

Thinking of Johnny, she said, "Bina, I need a favor."

The skin on Bina's face hung more loosely than it had before Seth left. The wrinkles around her eyes were more pronounced. Yet her eyes themselves were as fierce as ever. She narrowed them cautiously.

"What now?"

"Would you mind baking some *rugelach*?"

"What? Someone else is having a birthday? Why must you bring baking to people who you hardly know? Such needless expense."

"I promised for a friend."

"Then you make them."

Samantha sighed. Bina could be so frustrating.

"I'm working. I don't have time."

"Pfft," Bina said. "I cooked for my whole village during the war. I had no choice but to learn."

"I can cook."

"Oi! Not the Jewish *vay*!"

"Will you or won't you?"

Talia chimed in. "Please, Bubba!"

Bina smiled as she patted Talia's small hand. "For you, *sheifale*, my little lamb, I'll do it." Her smile fell as she looked back at Samantha. "I'll need ingredients. And we're almost out of coal."

DEATH WAS a part of life for Haley, but when she returned each night to her top-floor apartment on Grove Street near Philips, she tried to leave her job back at the morgue. Some nights were easier than others.

Haley's housekeeper, Molly McPhail, greeted her in the front entrance as Haley shed her summer cardigan and straw hat, and hung them on the coat rack. The four flights of stairs had her breathing harder than usual. She blamed it on the heat.

Molly, her face flushed and glistening, agreed with the sentiment. "It's so darned hot." Even with the windows open, the humidity could be oppressive. "But I daren't complain because before you know it, it's winter."

Haley smiled. Over the last seven years Molly had become more of a companion than merely a house-keeper. In fact, she had become a friend. "I quite agree," Haley said reassuringly. "Spring and fall are the only tolerable seasons."

The French doors that led to the living room on the right were wide open to allow for the flow of air. The high-ceilinged walls were neatly wallpapered and trimmed with dark wood. The furniture nestled around a cleaned-out stone fireplace, and tall west-facing windows brightened the room. Several flour-ishing plants dotted the apartment including a hanging Boston Fern and a four-foot-tall Areca Palm. A formidable polished-wood radio took a prominent posi-tion in the corner.

Molly's black three-legged cat stretched languidly on the plush maroon sofa taking up two seats. He raised a head at Haley's intrusion and narrowed his yellow eyes disapprovingly. Molly had christened him Mr. Midnight Caller for the time of day she'd discov-ered him at the fire escape, damp from the rain and thin from hunger. She'd had trouble sleeping and meant to heat a little milk to help her drift off when she heard the soft meowing. She'd brought the cat inside and shared her warm milk with him, and that was it. The cat had captured Molly's heart, and had never spent another day hungry or alone. They'd never know what had happened to his missing foot, but such trauma had been long forgotten. The feline was now plump and properly indignant in the way only cats could be. Haley spared a moment to rub him behind the ears which triggered a round of loud purring.

"I've got a nice potato and sausage casserole on, whenever you're ready," Molly said.

Haley's stomach growled at the mention of food. "I'm ready now."

On the sideboard was a framed photo of Haley's family. Her parents, now deceased, had been farmers in Brookline. Haley was the lone daughter amongst three sons, Benjamin, Harley-James, and Joseph. Joe's murder was what had triggered Haley's sudden departure from London where she'd been studying medicine. Joe's body had been discovered in an alley by a delivery boy in the early morning hours on a wet day in September of 1924. He'd been beaten up and ultimately killed by a knife to the throat. Detective Cluney had been the lead on the case—it was how Haley and the detective had first met—but even by his best efforts and Haley's amateur investigation, Joe's murder had never been solved.

The truth was, most murder cases weren't. Statistically, a mere one in ten saw a conviction in New York City, and Boston wasn't far behind.

The kitchen was warm and inviting with bright white walls and wooden cabinets painted a soothing sage-green. Approaching the sturdy wooden table, Haley sat in one of the matching chairs. "Smells delicious."

After they'd dished out their portions, Molly had said grace which was a concession Haley didn't mind making, even though the prayer was Catholic. Haley had been raised Episcopalian but had found that over the years her work had eclipsed her devotion to her religion.

Molly asked, "Anything interesting happen at work today?"

The twinkle in Molly's eye raised Haley's suspicions. "Is it in the newspapers already?"

"Aye. Evening edition of the *Daily Record*. A shooting on Union Street."

"I want to see it."

Molly shifted her weight off the chair and returned with the paper. "Here you go, Dr. Higgins," she said as she handed it to Haley. It was already unfolded with the story ready.

Haley read aloud, "An unidentified man was shot and killed in the Bell in Hand Tavern . . ." then finished the piece in silence until she came to the byline. "Sam Hawke."

"Do you know him?" Molly asked.

"Sam is short for Samantha. I just met her today. She seems driven." *Even desperate*, Haley thought, but kept that opinion to herself.

"A woman newspaper man?" Molly said.

"Well, I imagine she prefers newspaper *woman*," Haley said. "And it shouldn't be so shocking. Women, though few, are stepping into professions dominated by men. Like mine, for example."

"So right," Molly said. "So right." She chewed another piece of sausage, then asked, "Is it the Irish mob?"

Haley hesitated. "It could be."

"Or the Italian Mafia?"

"Possibly. But the shot that killed him came from within the tavern, not the shooting from the automobile."

"What does Detective Cluney say?"

"He believes it was the mob, probably Irish or Jewish since the victim was Italian. And he might be right. Conveniently, there's not a witness to confirm a shooter had entered the tavern, though in my opinion, the evidence speaks for itself."

Molly shifted from her seat and collected the dirty dishes. "Did the new medical examiner arrive today? I believe you mentioned a Dr. Guthrie."

"Yes, he did. Surprisingly, we've met before. Years ago, back in England."

"In England? Oh. Did he know our dear Mrs. Reed?"

Mrs. Georgia Reed, (nee Hartigan and the former Lady Gold, known to her friends and family as Ginger), Haley's dear friend, had resided in Boston in one of the prestigious brownstones facing the Common. Molly had been Ginger's maid until Ginger moved to London in 1923.

"Yes," Haley began, "Dr. Guthrie worked on a case that she and I were involved with."

"What's he like, then?" Molly asked, ever curious.

"Quirky fellow. He's tall with sharp angles—elbows, knees, even his chin. A mass of white wavy hair sprouts straight up off his head." Haley's hand flew to her head in demonstration. "Not much of a talker, either, except to complain, but very intelligent."

"We should invite him over for dinner," Molly said.

Haley groaned inwardly. "I suppose you're right. I'll ask him for a time that suits him."

The doorbell rang, and Haley's eyebrows lifted. "Are we expecting someone?"

Molly was already on her feet. "Not that I know of."

Before long Haley heard the sound of Molly opening the front door and then her voice shrilling. "Mr. and Mrs. Higgins! What a surprise!"

Haley jumped to her feet.

"Ben!" she said. She approached her eldest brother and gave him a quick embrace. Then to her sister-in-law Lorene, "Welcome. Come on in."

"Thanks, Sis." Belatedly, Ben removed his hat

revealing thinning brown hair and a receding hairline. Worry lines were etched around dark eyes and deeply grooved across his forehead. "We were in the neighborhood and thought we should stop in."

"We hope we aren't interrupting," Lorene said. Ben's wife was solidly built and the no-nonsense type that was well suited for life on the farm. "We should've called first."

"It's fine," Haley said. "We're happy to have you."

"We're just eating supper," Molly said. "You must join us."

"Yes, yes," Haley added. She had been just about to extend the offer as well.

Ben had never been one to say no to a free meal. He glanced at his wife who nodded subtly in approval.

Once they settled around the table and Ben and Lorene had been dished out the remaining casserole, Haley asked, "So, what brings you into Boston?"

Ben shared a look with his wife, then answered, "Picking up a new pig trough. Old one's rusting right through."

The way Lorene shifted uncomfortably made Haley think there was more to it than that but didn't feel it was her place to pry. Conversation was kept light, focusing on the plight of American farmers and the eternal question of when did they think the Depression would end.

"We're some of the fortunate ones," Ben said. "Our soil is staying put. Those poor fellas in the

Midwest are watching their farms blow away in the wind."

What they didn't talk about, what they never talked about, was their brother Joseph and his violent death.

Brother Harley-James was a safer topic.

"We haven't heard a peep from him," Lorene said. "Not that we get much for mail other than bills these days."

Haley commiserated. "I just hope he's keeping out of trouble."

Ben scoffed. "Knowing HJ, I doubt it."

It was true. Harley-James had been the one who got into schoolyard scraps and had frequent after school detentions. He was the one who'd gotten into bad company and trouble with the law.

Not Joseph. Joseph was thoughtful and kind, the type of fellow who'd give a stranger the shirt off his back.

It shouldn't have been Joseph.

Haley swallowed back the bitterness.

They finished their meal and Molly started to clear the table.

"Delicious meal, Molly," Lorene said. "Thank you."

Ben patted his stomach. "Yes, thank you."

"Would you like tea or coffee?" Haley asked.

"Actually, we should hit the road," Ben said. "We hate to eat and run, but the cows need milking."

"Of course," Haley said. "I completely understand. It was so nice of you to drop in."

As the couple was preparing to make their departure, Lorene gave Ben a long look. "Oh," Ben said, "I need to check the oil. You ladies can visit a little longer."

Ben disappeared abruptly, leaving Haley, Lorene, and Molly standing in his wake. Molly, being the intuitive type, excused herself. "I've got to get those dishes washed."

Haley guided Lorene to the living room and motioned for her to sit. She asked kindly, "Is everything all right? You seem bothered about something."

Even though they were alone in the room, Lorene leaned forward and lowered her voice. "The real reason we came into town was to see a ladies' doctor. Ben and I want a family. We've been married for almost three years and nothing." The look on her softly lined face grew earnest. "You're a doctor, Haley. Is there anything I can do? Ben wants a son."

Haley sympathized with the desperation in her sister-in-law's eyes. Barrenness was a terrible burden. Unfortunately, there weren't any miracle cures.

"Stress doesn't help," she said. "Try to relax."

"But how can I? I *want* a baby!"

The desire for motherhood resonated from Lorene in desperate waves.

Haley gently asked her, "Have you considered adoption?"

Lorene sighed. "We really want a child of our own. But, it's been so long, and I'm not getting any younger. I'll discuss the possibility with Ben."

Haley reassured her sister-in-law that this was a good idea. With the Depression worsening, more and more children were being abandoned and neglected with fewer families willing to take them in.

Ben knocked on the door and called for his wife. Lorene pinched back tears and took a deep breath. The window of emotional intimacy closed and propriety took its place. "Thank you so much for your hospitality, Haley," he said. "Dinner was fabulous."

As Haley waved them off she couldn't help but feel like she'd failed somehow.

She escaped to her home office where she spent time studying when not at work. It was a sanctuary of sorts, and she purposely hadn't installed a telephone. The top of her small ornate wooden desk was cleared off, with only a reading lamp and the latest science magazine sitting upon it. Haley picked up a putting iron propped up in one corner. The sparsely furnished room had space for another of her passions: golf, a sport she'd taken up a year after she'd moved back to Boston. The concentration needed to excel forced her to clear her mind of work and other worries. She set a golf ball on the artificial putting hole she'd set up in the middle of the room.

The ringing of the telephone from the kitchen

reached her just as she completed her fifth hole-in-one shot.

Moments later Molly tapped on the door and stepped inside, her expression serious. "Detective Cluney wants you to meet him at twenty-nine Endicott. There's been another death."

5

The address Molly had given Haley would be a long walk to get to, so Haley started up the DeSoto and headed northeast to the edge of the Jewish neighborhood. She knew the place—no one in the North End didn't. Madame Mercier's "home of ill repute" was quite renowned and somehow managed to break a dozen laws without the hammer coming down. This included gambling, imbibing of alcohol, and of course, intimate relations for a fee.

Madame Mercier's clientele had money and often prestige, and included members of the police and those who held public office. Detective Cluney said he'd called Haley instead of Dr. Guthrie because he knew Haley would be discreet. Detective Cluney didn't know Dr. Guthrie well enough to say the same about him, and Haley didn't yet know the answer to that either.

The officer at the door told her the body was upstairs. Haley nodded and headed up.

Housed in an old two-story townhouse, the brothel looked a lot better on the inside than out. While the bricks on the exterior crumbled, the décor on the inside —including the wallpaper, furniture, and area rugs— was a mix of deep reds and gold and was notably of good quality. While the outside of the house wouldn't inspire a passing glance, the inside was designed to provoke the wealthy.

Detective Cluney stood on the landing. "Thanks for coming this time of the evening." His eyes widened at Haley's windblown look. She pushed curls behind her ears. "You didn't walk here, did you?" he said.

"No. I drove my car. With the windows down."

Cluney snorted in approval. "The body's in here."

Several women dressed in knee-length, thin silk or satin chemises, some trimmed with white or pink downy feathers, lined the hallway. Well-coiffed heads poked upward in an effort to see, with worry—real or pretend, Haley couldn't tell—on their heavily made-up faces. One, Haley was surprised to notice, had a large, protruding stomach, and was obviously expecting a child.

The room was also a mix of reds and gold with a wooden four-poster bed fitted with white sheets and a matching white summer quilt. Feathers littered the wooden dresser, the night table, and fell to the dark wood floor.

A semi-naked girl lay on her back, a bullet hole to her head. Haley sighed. Two shooting deaths in one day.

"What's her name?"

"They call her Snowflake," Detective Cluney said, but the madam says the girl's real name is Agnes O'Reilly."

Haley put her black medical bag on the floor, removed her gloves, and took the girl's wrists. Her body was warm to the touch. The room itself was overly warm, which made it difficult to pinpoint the time of death.

"Looks like a trick gone wrong," Detective Cluney announced. He removed a hankie from his suit pocket and mopped his face. He returned the used piece of linen to its home then removed his straw hat.

"Detective, who found the body?" she asked.

A female voice answered, "Chantilly."

The woman, who appeared to be in her forties, entered the room. Unlike the girls lining the hall, she wore a full-length Japanese kimono tied snugly around a narrow waist. Her blond hair showed signs of gray and the lines around her eyes and lips were well established. Despite this, she was a very attractive woman.

Haley wagered a guess. "Madame Mercier?"

"Zee von and only." The woman's French accent was not Parisian. After her time in France during the war, Haley knew a continental French accent when she heard one. French Canadian maybe? Or possibly she was from the French Quarter of New Orleans.

Madame Mercier held Haley's gaze in a manner that projected that she was the one in charge in this house. She looked away before making strides toward the electric fan, but Haley stopped her. "No, please. Don't turn it on. It could ruin the evidence."

"Verry vell." She folded her arms defiantly over her chest. "As I said, Chantilly found Snowflake."

"Bring this Chantilly gal in," Detective Cluney directed.

Chantilly—not her real name Haley assumed—was a slight woman with dull eyes and crimson lips. Detective Cluney cleared his throat, and Haley was amused to see his neck reddening with discomfort.

"Hello," Haley said kindly. "I'm Dr. Higgins. We understand you found Snowflake. Can you tell us what happened leading up to your discovery?"

Chantilly's slender hand reached for her throat. "I wanted to ask her something, she was my friend, you see, and I knew she had, uh, a guest. So I waited. But when time went on, and she never came out, I tried the door. It wasn't locked, so I went in."

Detective Cluney found his voice. "Did you touch anything?"

"Only the pillow."

"What pillow?"

"The one on her face."

Haley and the detective shared a look. There was

one pillow on the bed, and Haley pointed to it. "That pillow?"

"No, ma'am." Chantilly glanced at another pillow now partially under the bed. "It must've fallen to the floor. I lifted it off her face, and that's when I started screaming. I must've dropped it then."

Haley leaned over to look under the bed and saw the edge of the pillow there. She grabbed it and lifted it. A big, round hole was blown through the middle of it.

"That would account for all the feathers," she said.

Detective Cluney stated the obvious. "The killer held the pillow over her face and shot her clear through it." He stepped into the hallway. "Anyone hear a gunshot?"

Haley couldn't see the girls but guessed they shook their heads in the negative when the detective repeated his question.

"No one?" he bellowed.

"Vee make a habit of playing ze gramophone at a raazer high volume," Madame Mercier purred in her French accent. "For privacy's sake."

"The pillow would've muffled the gunshot," Haley said.

Detective Cluney called for one of his officers. "Get the body to the morgue."

Haley scanned the room looking for a gun. Something glinted from the light of the gas lamp. Haley picked up the item, held it between two fingers and showed it to Detective Cluney.

"It's a bullet casing," she said. "We should get it to the police lab for examination." By *we*, Haley meant *him*, but the nuance was lost on the detective.

"Knock yourself out." He said it in a way that made Haley believe that not much was going to be done to find Snowflake's killer. Prostitutes weren't worth spending taxpayer's money on.

Once the body was removed, there'd be no need for staying behind, but Haley was reluctant to go. No matter what this girl had done for a living, she was a human being who deserved justice. There had to be a clue somewhere. She scoured the room, wishing she had a photographic memory

A commotion came from the bottom of the stairs, and a familiar voice reached her.

"Is Dr. Higgins here?"

Haley hurried to the landing and stared at the blond woman fighting her way past the officer at the door. "I'm with the *Boston Daily Record*, and I insist you let me see the doctor if she's here."

Haley noted the messenger bag strapped over Miss Hawke's shoulder, and that she also carried another bulkier case. "Please let her in."

"I must insist that she doesn't!" Madame Mercier said. "I can't have theese unfortunate event become a story in the papers. It's bad for business!"

"She won't write a story, I promise," Haley said,

ignoring Samantha Hawke's sharp look. She motioned for the journalist to come up. Without a greeting, she said quietly. "I don't suppose you have a camera in there."

"I do. It's just a box camera. It doesn't have a flash."

The long days of June meant there would be sufficient light to make the photographs.

"It'll do. Please, as fast as you can, take pictures. They'll be here soon to move the body, and then the scene will be compromised."

Haley was pleased to see that Miss Hawke didn't faint at the sight of blood or become rattled by the dead body in the room. Some people could write about violence but were unable to stomach it in real life.

Once Miss Hawke had her gear ready, Haley gave instructions. "The body, of course, several angles please, then the room from all four corners.

Just as they heard the gurney knocking about as it was lifted up the stairs, they finished the deed.

"Good," Haley said. "We can go."

Samantha Hawke packed the camera. "Are you going to explain to me why I'm not writing a story?"

"In my car. I'll drive you home."

"Uh, that's not necessary."

Haley heard the hesitation in Miss Hawke's voice. "It'll save you taxi fare. Plus, I want to know how you happened upon Madame Mercier's abode when murder had been committed."

THE LAST THING Samantha wanted was for Dr. Higgins to learn where she lived. It was hard enough to get the respect of your peers, much less someone as sophisticated and educated as Dr. Haley Higgins.

"No, really," she said. "It's fine. I was visiting a friend and saw the police. I came out of curiosity." Even to Samantha's ears, her words sounded like an excuse. She couldn't very well say that she lived one street over in a run-down tenement building and had seen the police lights from her living room window. She'd almost had to fight Bina off when she grabbed her bags and headed out.

"You're going to get yourself killed and then what will happen to us!" she'd declared. "You're *meshugge*." Crazy. "Your child will be an orphan!"

"I'll be fine," Samantha had insisted. When her adrenaline was up, she always felt invincible. "I won't be long, I promise."

She'd better keep that promise if she didn't want to spend the night listening to Bina's reprimands, first in English and again in Yiddish.

She spoke quickly to Dr. Higgins. "I'll develop the film tomorrow and deliver the photographs to the morgue myself. I have to go. Bye!" She scampered into the deepening twilight before the doctor could protest.

Samantha ran through the alley, her bravado dissipating with the hot breeze that blew along the brick walls of the narrow street. Every snap or cat's meow was a warning she wasn't alone. She was relieved when she finally stepped into her tenement in one piece, with only Bina's wrath to face.

Bina sat in an armchair wearing her nightclothes with her hair in curlers and lips so tight they almost disappeared.

"I'm back," Samantha said. "You can go to bed now."

Bina's scowl deepened as she pushed herself out of the chair. "I hope that was worth it," she said, before disappearing into her room, her nose high with righteous indignation.

Samantha checked on Talia. Her daughter looked like an angel sleeping there. Everything she did was for Talia's sake. Even the risks she took. But Bina was right. She should be careful. Talia had already lost one parent.

Thoughts of Seth Rosenbaum had Samantha unlocking the sideboard cupboard. She poured herself a short glass of bootlegged whiskey and pinched up her face as the poison burned its way down. If only she could afford the real stuff the rum runners brought to shore from Canada or Britain. This rot was from someone's backyard bathtub. But it took the edge off and was better than nothing.

Claiming her camera, Samantha snuck out the fire escape. Long ago she'd discovered the space in the attic above their apartment and had set up a makeshift darkroom there. So far no one had discovered it, and if they had, they'd left her chemicals and soaking trays alone. Before blocking the light with a thick woolen blanket, she turned on the large flashlight she'd equipped with a red bulb.

Samantha could've taken the film to the office and used the darkroom there, but then she'd have to explain what she had, and that would force her to break her promise to Dr. Higgins to not write a story. Samantha was one hundred percent sure news of the prostitute's death wouldn't make any of the city's papers. The editors would call it a waste of ink. No, if she wanted this story, it had to be bigger than a bad trick. Something in her gut told her there was more to it than met the eye. Why else would Dr. Higgins be so keen on getting photographs?

Samantha waited until the images bloomed on the white developing paper and then pinned them to the string she'd hung between the rafters. In the calming glow of the red illumination, she studied the photographs.

There was a big story here. Samantha could feel it in her guts. If only she could see where.

6

The next morning, Haley found Dr. Guthrie sitting still at his desk. Haley's pulse skipped a beat. Perhaps *too* still? The chief medical examiner was approaching his golden years, Haley guessed late sixties, and that was being conservative. She wondered again how an elderly foreigner had managed to snag this coveted position. He must have been well acquainted with someone in power. Haley didn't know if she'd ever find out because she certainly wasn't about to ask him.

She tiptoed toward Dr. Guthrie whose pointy chin was resting on his chest. If the man was breathing, it was shallow.

"Dr. Guthrie?"

Haley tapped him on the shoulder, and the man jumped, startling them both.

"What the dickens?" He seared her with a look of accusation. "What on earth possessed you to sneak up on me like that?"

Haley blushed, feeling a little foolish. "You were asleep. I only meant to wake you."

"Well, I'm awake now. Perhaps you can make amends by making me a proper pot of tea. I gather you learned how to during your time in London living with the posh."

Haley stared back with disapproval. She was beginning to miss the former chief medical examiner immensely. However, though she preferred a strong Italian coffee, her time in London had conditioned her to enjoy tea as well.

Dr. Guthrie's mood cheered once Haley delivered the tea. She was about to leave the man to his musings, and what looked like the crossword puzzle in the *Boston Daily Record*, when her thoughts returned to Agnes O'Reilly, known by her associates as Snowflake.

"Is there anything in the paper about last night's death?" she asked.

Dr. Guthrie's bushy eyebrows inched up. "The woman with the gunshot wound?"

"Yes."

The doctor grunted. "Not that I saw."

Haley was both pleased and annoyed. Pleased that Miss Hawke had kept her promise. For some reason that surprised her. Her actions didn't line up with

Haley's impression of the hardworking, driven journalist.

Even so, Haley couldn't help feeling annoyed that the shooting death of a blue-collar man was considered news, making it into the evening papers, while the shooting death of a "blue-collar" woman was not. Sam Hawke had kept her word and hadn't reported it, but she wasn't the only newshound around.

Haley sipped her tea as she took in the morgue. The surgical table was empty. She called to Dr. Guthrie who could hear her through his opened office door. "Should I prepare the body for the postmortem?"

Through the glass, Haley watched Dr. Guthrie work his lips. "I imagine you are speaking of the female that came in last night?"

Obviously. "Yes, doctor."

"Whatever for? Cause of death is evident. Why waste taxpayers' money on a corpse destined to be buried in the paupers' graveyard?"

Haley nearly choked on her tea. "Because the woman was murdered! An autopsy might provide clues to the killer."

Dr. Guthrie harrumphed. "I doubt the mayor cares about that."

Okay, first clue to how Dr. Guthrie got this job. He was friendly with the mayor.

"Well, I care!"

Dr. Guthrie seemed to be considering Haley carefully—she could practically see the wheels turning in his head thinking that the mayor was one thing, but he had to work with this hysterical woman.

"Very well," he finally said. "You may proceed with the autopsy of Agnes O'Reilly, but only because we're not presently busy, and I wouldn't want a disagreement to grow between us unnecessarily."

Haley's lips twitched. She had the feeling that Mrs. Guthrie had been a formidable lady.

Haley donned her lab coat, opened the refrigerated cabinet marked O'Reilly, pulled the chilled corpse out, and pushed the trolley to the surgical table. After washing her hands with soap in the nearby sink, she carefully shifted Miss O'Reilly from the trolley to the table then turned on the electric lamp that hung overhead.

She started the routine: Y incision, examination of the vital organs, collection of the stomach contents.

The uterus appeared enlarged. Haley reined in her emotions as she made the incision to open it up. She wasn't surprised by what she found there.

Later, once she'd completed the task, Haley reported to Dr. Guthrie, "Miss O'Reilly was pregnant."

"I suppose that happens from time to time in her profession," was all he said.

Haley thought of the other girl, Primrose, who was also expecting. Surely Madame Mercier taught her girls about birth control? There were options available for women nowadays.

The morgue telephone rang, and when Dr.

Guthrie saw that Haley was in no position to pick it up, he grunted and strode to the apparatus himself. He had a way of walking that suggested there were unsavory obstacles in his path, and it required lifting his knees unusually high. Haley almost chuckled out loud.

"The detective wants the report on the Marchesi fellow," Dr. Guthrie stated. "You don't mind running it over, do you?"

The police station shared a backyard border with the hospital, and wasn't so far that Dr. Guthrie couldn't make the jaunt. But Haley was happy to do it. She needed fresh air and a chance to clear her head.

The police officer at the front counter directed Haley to Detective Cluney's desk. On it was a telephone, a stack of papers, an ashtray due to be emptied, and a framed photograph of his family—a wife and four kids. The detective set a half-empty coffee mug down when he saw Haley approach.

"Ah, Dr. Higgins," he said. "No doubt our new chief medical examiner's not keen on the heat and humidity. My guess is his visits will be more infrequent than the former ME's."

"I suspect you might be right about that," Haley said. She handed over the manila envelope.

Detective Cluney perused the contents. "Ah-ha. As I expected. A bullet killed him."

Haley cocked a head at the detective's snide tone. "But which bullet?"

The detective clipped the tip of a cigar, clamped it

between dry lips as he lit it, and blew smoke out the side of his mouth, away from where Haley stood: a courtesy she appreciated.

"Like we determined at the scene, there was no bullet casing found in the teahouse, however, since we last spoke, a new witness has come forward. A bum camped out across the street. Says a man in a long brown trench coat entered the Bell in Hand just minutes before a *backfired,* and then exited seconds afterward." He inhaled and then tapped ash into the ashtray. "Can't say how reliable his word is."

"It's interesting that both he and the waiter mentioned a car backfiring."

The detective extinguished his half-smoked cigar. "Cars backfire all the time."

"Have you learned anything more about the victim?" Haley asked. She knew her questions about the case were beyond the scope of her jurisdiction as the forensic pathologist—she was there to give information not ask for it—but she and Detective Cluney had developed a semi-comfortable professional relationship over the years. Haley believed he respected her input and opinions since she'd helped him solve more than one case in the past.

The detective waved at an empty wooden chair. "You might as well sit down, Dr. Higgins."

Haley accepted his offer, and the detective continued.

"Stefano Marchesi was what you might call the

black sheep of the family. Broke ties with their Mob dealings, determined to make his own way."

"Interesting," Haley said. "Here's a man who could have anything he wanted as far as earthly comforts and pleasures go, and yet he chooses to make it on his own? He either had upstanding moral character, or there's more to the story."

"I'd bet on more to the story," Detective Cluney said, then quickly added, "hypothetically of course."

"So what did Mr. Marchesi do to make his living?"

"Fisherman."

Haley studied Detective Cluney's face. Nowadays, a man who claimed to fish, usually supplemented his income by rum running.

"Did he have his own boat?"

"Indeed, he did."

"'Curiouser and curiouser,'" Haley mused.

Detective Cluney's thick forehead buckled. "What?"

"It's a quote from *Alice's Adventures in Wonderland*," Haley explained.

"Bah," Detective Cluney said dismissively. He picked up his discarded cigar butt and relit it. "I only read the papers."

Haley waited a moment, hoping Detective Cluney would ask about the death of the girl from the brothel, but when he didn't, she said, "I performed the autopsy on the victim from last night."

"Huh? Oh, yeah. Let me guess. She died from a gunshot wound to the head."

Haley huffed. "Is that necessary? Autopsies can reveal more than just the obvious."

"My apologies, Dr. Higgins. What did you discover?"

"Well," Haley pushed a stray curl behind her ear. "She was with child."

"Another one?"

"You mean another of Madame Mercier's girls or another child?"

"Another prostitute knocked up."

"Yes," Haley said, ignoring the detective's brashness. "It could be motive."

"You think someone in a position of power might've been the father?"

"It's possible." Haley wished she had the photographs Samantha Hawke had taken. She didn't know what she could glean from them, but something niggled at her subconscious.

Detective Cluney stared at the yellowed, nicotine-stained ceiling, "Maybe. But not provable." He shrugged a thick shoulder and brought the conversation to an end by adding, "Thanks for dropping the report by."

Haley stood and smoothed the wrinkles out of her summer dress suit. "You're welcome. Have a good day, Detective."

Outside, Haley adjusted the brim of her hat to block the sun more effectively. Instead of walking toward the morgue, she headed in the direction of her parked car.

7

---

*B*ina had gotten up early to bake the *rugelach*, despite Samantha's insistence that the night before would be fine.

"Feh!" Bina had exclaimed at the dinner table the previous evening. "It's important that my *rugelach* are served fresh. Always the younger generation wants to take short cuts, take the easy way. The schmaltzy twenties made you soft! And now that times are hard again—"

With Bina, a simple yes or no would never do.

However, the morning smelled brighter and more promising with the mouth-watering sweet aroma of *rugelach* filling their small apartment.

"Mommy."

Talia stood in the hallway in too-small pajamas and wiped sleep out of her eyes with her little fist.

"Good morning, sweet one."

Samantha couldn't resist scooping her up into her arms. "*Oof*, you're getting so big, I can barely lift you!"

Talia snuggled her nose into her mother's neck and Samantha breathed in deeply the smell of her young daughter.

Talia's breath tickled Samantha's ear. "Can I have *rugelach* for breakfast?"

"Of course."

Talia wiggled out of Samantha's arms and raced for the kitchen. Samantha burst out laughing as she watched her go. "Such a wild thing, you are."

Later, in the newsroom, Samantha immediately had the attention of her co-workers when they realized what it was that she carried on the platter in her arms.

The anticipation was enough to make shy Max speak aloud. "You made *rugelach*?"

Samantha felt a little bit guilty when once again she never corrected Max's assumption.

"Doll!" Johnny said with a big grin. "I smelled something delicious the minute the door opened, and this time I'm not talking about you."

"You're such a tease, Johnny."

Samantha placed the tray of pastries by the coffee maker and removed the tea towel.

"Wait a minute," Johnny protested. "Those are my *rugelach*. You and I had a deal, sweet pea."

Samantha teased back. "Do you mean to say you won't share? The boys might end up fighting you for them, and I'm not sure you'd win."

The boys had indeed gathered around and pushed Johnny about playfully.

"You eat all that," Freddy Hall said, "and you'll get fat as a hog."

Another jumped in. "And sick too!"

"Fine," Johnny said, feigning defeat. "I'll share."

Samantha sat at her desk and watched the fellows, who resembled a group of hogs around the feeding trough, and she couldn't help but laugh.

"What in Hades is going on?"

Silence filled the room at Archie August's bellow, and they scampered back to their desks, wiping crumbs off their faces as they went.

The editor's beady eyes landed on the near-empty tray and spied the lone *rugelach* left among the remnants.

"Whose birthday?" he said, then walked over and claimed the last pastry. "Never mind," he mumbled with his mouth full. "Just get back to work."

He pivoted heavily to face Samantha. "Miss Hawke, my office."

Samantha's pulse jumped. What did the boss want with her? She patted her blond locks and wished she had a moment to apply more lipstick, but that was something she could never do in the company of men.

"Mr. August?" she said as she followed him. Mr. August wasn't sentimental, and his office was free of personal photographs or items of comfort. The walls were bare, though he could boast a window. Samantha wondered if the glass was ever cleaned and could hardly make out the streetscape below due to the buildup of grime. Small piles of papers, a variety of pens, and a well-used coffee mug littered the editor's desk. A partially smoked cigar rested in an overfull ashtray.

"Take a seat, Miss Hawke."

"Is something wrong?" Samantha mentally assessed her work and nothing contrary came to mind.

"Not at all. I wanted to commend you on your piece about the tavern death. You didn't mind tagging along with Johnny? I know it's muggy outside."

"Not at all," Samantha said automatically, then her thoughts backtracked. *You didn't mind tagging along with Johnny?*

That son of a gun! Some deal he'd made! And a fool out of her, traipsing to work all thankful for Johnny's offer when it had been Mr. August's offer all along. And a tray of *rugelach* to boot!

"*The Globe* has a female reporter now," she heard Mr. August say when she'd tethered her anger. "I thought I should give you a chance."

Aha. Mr. August meant to keep up with the Joneses.

"I appreciate it, sir," Samantha said. "And I won't let you down."

"I'm sure. This means you're free to go out on the beat with the guys or on your own."

"Yes, sir!"

"But you're still in charge of the ladies' pages."

Samantha figured as much. She returned to her desk without giving Johnny a sideways glance. Two could play at his game.

She reviewed her files. She was working on stories about the glamorous Joan Crawford, and how to sew a dress using a bias cut. And the piece on Dr. Higgins. Thinking about the assistant medical examiner reminded Samantha about the photos now hidden between her mattresses. She'd spent an hour studying them but for the life of her, could find nothing that could point to the killer. Dr. Higgins had been adamant that the photographs be taken before the body was whisked away. What was it that she'd seen? Or that she thought she'd seen?

Samantha should drop the photographs off today, but she wanted one more opportunity to look at them first, this time in the light of day, and she wouldn't have that chance until she took her lunch break. She normally ate at the desk. With Talia in school, it meant only Bina was at the apartment and, well, they didn't exactly enjoy one another's company.

Then there was Archie August and his newfound faith in her. She knew she'd get sacked if he ever found out she had them and hadn't brought them to the paper. Prostitute or not, if it was a potential lead, he wanted it.

Samantha worked on the ladies' pieces until she

was ready to go. Johnny approached as she was putting on her coat.

"Are you heading to the wharves?"

"What?"

"August, he told you, didn't he?"

"I don't know what you're talking about," Samantha said stiffly.

"Ah, don't be sore. All the guys appreciated the *rugelach*, not just me. And besides, you want the guys to like having you around, right? You know Freddy's not the only nut needin' crackin'."

Incredulous, Samantha stared at the infuriating man. "What I want is to be taken seriously."

"We do," Johnny insisted. "*I* do. Look here, why don't we go to the docks together." He raised his palms. "Not that you need protecting or anything like, just you know, two heads are better than one."

Samantha pretended to consider his offer while congratulating herself on getting in on Johnny's lead while he thought Mr. August had given it to her.

"Okay, fine. But you're driving."

Johnny jiggled his keys in the air. "Whatever you say, boss."

HALEY DIDN'T KNOW what she had expected to find, but her curiosity—morbid, perhaps—drew her back to the scene of the crime. The one at the Bell in Hand.

Traffic moved slowly down Union Street as Haley followed a white van advertising Coca-Cola in large red script that was inching along ahead of her. Traffic could be bad this time of day, especially on the busier Hanover Street they were merging onto. The slow pace allowed her to take a good look at the damaged windows, several covered in sheets of plywood while another was being replaced by three men who belonged to the work truck parked nearby.

Once parked, Haley searched for the homeless man opposite the tavern whom Detective Cluney had mentioned, but could find no evidence of him.

She half expected the heavy wooden door to the tavern to be locked, but it opened with a slight complaint from the hinges.

There were a few customers seated at a table near the door, but the back of the room where the killing had occurred was roped off. She strolled toward the barrier and shuffled underneath the rope as if she had every right to do it.

Someone had swept and mopped up the blood and Haley silently groaned. At least she had witnessed the police photographer taking plenty of photographs. If she asked nicely, Detective Cluney might let her see them.

The window with the crucial bullet hole was one of the ones boarded up, and Haley took another look at the crater. She confirmed for her own sake the direction of the glass shards. The rim of the one from the bullet that had killed Stefano Marchesi moved outward. The bullet had definitely been shot from inside. She compared it with the others, and the directional position of the shards pointed inward. Those shots came from outside. There was no way Detective Cluney could reasonably deny the evidence.

Haley studied the floor and bent to look under the table. She examined the chair, then sighed. She'd hoped to discover something new, but it appeared to be a waste of time.

"Hey! You're not supposed to be there."

The voice belonged to the waiter, Mr. Tobin. He stood on the other side of the bar, hands hidden behind the counter.

"Oh, it's you," he said as recognition dawned.

"I'm sorry," Haley began contritely. "I should've asked for permission first."

Mr. Tobin shrugged. "What did ya hope to find?"

"I wish I knew." Haley stepped toward the man, keeping a smile on her face. "I see they didn't arrest you."

Mr. Tobin scoffed. "It weren't like they didn't try. But they had nothin' on me. Cuz, I didn't do anything."

"I didn't think you did," Haley said, not quite truthfully. "The police are just doing their job."

"And a damn poor one at that."

Haley softened the muscles in her face and commiserated. "Soon it will be over."

Mr. Tobin's shoulders loosened, and the tightness in his face eased. "Ya, hope so."

"I know you're probably tired of answering questions," Haley said, "but would you mind answering a few for me?"

"I guess so, though I'd like to know why you care?"

"The answer to that is simple, and, I admit, rather vain. I like puzzles. If you recall, I'm the assistant to the chief medical examiner. The first puzzle for me is the postmortem. I examined and weighed Mr. March's vital organs, including the brain, which I later dissected. His stomach contents revealed that he'd eaten beef stew about an hour before coming here for tea. An autopsy often helps when it comes to determining cause and time of death and establishing other details of the victim's health prior to his death. In this man's case, it was quite obvious that the cause of death was a gunshot to the heart. Rather close range, I'd say, and I'm convinced, from inside this restaurant."

Mr. Tobin stared wide-eyed at Haley's graphic description. His freckled face had grown pale, and somehow Haley couldn't imagine this young man pulling the trigger. However, she'd been surprised before.

Swallowing thickly, Mr. Tobin said, "Okay."

Assuming that was his answer to her question about his answering a few for her, she dove in. "Did you know the man who dined here?"

Mr. Tobin shook his head. "No, ma'am."

"You're sure? He'd never patronized the Bell in Hand before?"

"Well, yeah, he'd come in. I know his *name*, but I don't know him. I don't know a lot of the people who drink, I mean *eat*, here. I keep to my own business if you know what I mean. It's good for my health."

"I know you said that Mr. March was alone in the tavern at the time of his death. There's a witness who says he saw a second man in a trench coat come in around that time. Does that ring any bells?"

"Like I said, I didn't see no one, but that doesn't mean nobody came in. I could've been in the kitchen or storage room, or busy behind the counter here."

"I see. Do you ever have impoverished people come in?"

"We're no charity, ma'am. If a fella don't have any cash, we show him the door."

Haley pointed toward the newly replaced window. "Ever see someone hanging around across the street?"

"Ol' Oscar? Sometimes. Why? Is he the guy who said a fella came in and shot Mr. March?"

"I can't say for certain."

"Well, he's crazy, ma'am. Spins yarns like no other. You can't believe a word he says."

8

The distance between the *Daily Record* and the wharves on Atlantic Avenue was only half a mile, and Johnny's two-seater, cherry-red Packard Roadster—hardly a covert machine, Samantha thought—rumbled along State Street past the court-house where the view of the Boston Channel opened wide.

The temperature hovered in the mid-eighties, and the reflection of the sun off the harbor was tear-inducing. Samantha opened her purse and removed a pair of sunglasses—a fantastic invention designed by a fellow named Foster from Atlantic City—and put them on.

Johnny whistled. "You look like a Hollywood film star."

"You're just jealous."

Johnny chuckled as he parked his vehicle at Long

Wharf. "As a matter of fact, I am. Where does a fellow go to buy a pair?"

"I got mine from Sears."

They climbed out of the vehicle and Samantha pressed down on the bell-shaped cloche hat on her head. She'd owned the thing for years now and vowed she'd buy a newer style as soon as her ship came in. Surely, if she broke a big story, Mr. August would be willing to give her a raise.

Samantha didn't know for certain why she and Johnny were standing on the docks, except that Mr. August had tipped Johnny off and had failed to do the same for her. She assumed that they were to follow up on the death of Mr. Marchesi, alias March, but she wasn't about to ask Johnny.

Before long, Johnny answered her unspoken question.

"Stephen March was a fisherman," he said. "Somebody here must know who he was." He tipped his hat further down on his face as if to block the glare of the sun dancing on the canal. "If we're really lucky, someone will know the guy's darkest secrets too."

Samantha wasn't sure what they were supposed to do next. This was the first time, except for the murder she'd happened upon at the brothel, she'd been out on the beat investigating a news story. Again she stayed quiet and followed Johnny's lead. He'd done this kind of thing hundreds of times, and if Samantha was anything, she was a quick learner.

Johnny pointed. "There are some hardworking fellas. Let's start there."

Samantha fell into step with her long-legged co-worker and nearly slipped on the slick surface of the dock. Impulsively, she grabbed on to Johnny's arm.

"Whoa there, filly," Johnny said with a glint in his eyes.

Samantha wanted to sock him in the nose. "It's these darn heels," Samantha muttered. She released her grip on Johnny and jutted her chin out. "Life is so much easier for men."

She stared at two fellows on the dock hoisting heavy cases of who-knew-what onto the back of a truck, then as they returned to the boat, pressed dirty hands at the base of their backs with a groan.

"I wonder if those guys feel the same way?" Johnny said.

As Samantha and Johnny drew closer, the men stopped what they were doing and stared. Both workers wore overalls, blue shirts rolled up to the biceps, and flat caps on their heads. Samantha couldn't help but notice that one of the men had a badly mangled ear.

The other one nodded his chin as Samantha and Johnny approached. Without smiling, he said, "I believe you folks are lost."

"We're looking for a man called March," Johnny said.

The fellow eyed them suspiciously. "What for?"

"Do you know him or not?" Johnny pressed.

"You a cop?"

"No. We're from the *Daily Record*. I'm Johnny Milwaukee, and this is Samantha Hawke."

The dockworker eyed Samantha up and down. "Takin' a man's job," he stated.

"And why not?" Samantha returned sharply. She was so sick of hearing this tired argument. "Tough times aren't just for men."

"You know our names," Johnny said. "How about returning the favor?"

"Bobby Ryan." His gaze darted back to his pal on the boat. "That's James Boyle."

"What are you unloading here?" Samantha asked.

Bobby Ryan squinted. "You're sure you're not cops?"

Johnny pulled out a wrinkled press pass from his suit pocket and flashed it. "We're not cops."

"Not that it matters," Bobby Ryan said. "Because we're all on the up and up here. Just fish, you see."

"About the guy, March," Johnny said.

"Oh. He didn't show up for work today, the dirty dog."

Johnny dislodged a piece of paper from his pocket and showed it to Mr. Ryan. It was a picture of the dead man, Stefano Marchesi.

"Is this the guy?"

Grim-faced, Bobby Ryan nodded. "Son of a gun."

He pulled out a home-rolled cigarette and deftly lit it with a match.

"You didn't read about his death in the papers?" Samantha asked.

Two streams of smoke trailed out of the man's nose. "Who's got time to read?"

Samantha ignored the man's ignorance. "How well did you know him? Were you friends?"

Johnny lowered the hammer. "Did you run rum together?"

Bobby Ryan chortled. "That's real swell."

"We're not cops," Samantha said again. She removed her sunglasses and smiled with both her mouth and her eyes. "You can remain anonymous, Mr. Ryan. We're only looking for a story and maybe help to find the killer. Wouldn't you like that?"

"No names?" Bobby Ryan said.

"No names. Besides prohibition is rarely enforced nowadays," Samantha said, hoping to alleviate Mr. Ryan's trepidation. "In fact, I predict the Eighteenth Amendment will be repealed in the near future."

Johnny shot her a surprised look but said nothing.

Bobby Ryan flashed an amused grin. "Now that'd be bad for business." He dropped his cigarette and squashed it with his boot. "Thing is, I don't know what to tell you that you don't already know. Canadian Whiskey, English Gin, and French Champagne. That's what Americans with taste want. They'll get it one way or another. We're just helping out a little. 'Cept, Stev —" Bobby Ryan frowned and glanced at Samantha and Johnny as if he regretted the sentence he'd started.

"I gotta get back to work."

"Except what, Mr. Ryan?" Samantha said. "What did Stephen March do?"

"Us runners got a code, you see. We don't cheat each other."

"Cheat how? How did Stephen March cheat?" Johnny said. "Money or women?"

Bobby Ryan stared hard before responding. "Both."

Exhilarated by the fact that she was pursuing a crime story, Samantha fought the smile that threatened to overtake her face as she slid into Johnny's car. Under no circumstances would she allow Johnny to see how thrilled she was. This kind of thing was old hat for him, and he wouldn't waste a moment before giving her a hard time if he knew.

"My bet," Johnny said wryly, "is poker. March cheated, took winnings he didn't deserve and was rubbed out cuz of it."

Keeping her tone as professional as possible, she said, "Sounds like motive to me. "

"Yup."

"Mr. March cheated Mr. Ryan, and now he's dead." Samantha was feeling pretty good about their investigation so far. Wouldn't it be something if she —they solved this case? It sure would be a feather in her cap; her first lead and the case was broken!

All they had to do was prove it.

Good thing Johnny couldn't read her mind.

He popped her bubble by saying, "Though my contact with the police says the commissioner's determined to write it up as a gang killing."

"Is that how you got that photograph?" Samantha said, feeling a bit miffed. She hated how she always felt behind the curve, especially when, for a fleeting second, she'd thought she was ahead.

Johnny confirmed with a nod. "Handy fella."

Samantha pursed her lips. The previous thrill of the chase she'd felt quickly sifted away. If she was going to play with the boys she'd need a police contact too, but how did a person go about doing that? She wasn't about to ask Johnny, that was for sure. Maybe Max? Yes, he'd know. If only she could get him to talk to her without him dying of embarrassment. He really ought to get over his fear of women. Maybe there was a way she could help with that.

"Can I see it?" she asked.

"Huh?"

"The photograph. I want to see it."

"It's pretty gruesome."

Samantha glared back hotly, and Johnny was smart enough to give her the photograph without another word.

Pinching the corner of the picture, Samantha gave it a good look. Stephen March was slumped over a booth table. A stain blossomed on the left side of a light-colored linen suit. His hat had fallen off and lay on the floor by his feet.

"He's dead, all right," was all she said. Admittedly, Samantha had no medical training. Dr. Higgins was sure to know more about it. She gave the photo back, and Johnny returned it to his suit pocket.

They were inching their way down Market Street by Faneuil Hall where the fishmongers weighed out the catch of the day and wrapped it in newspaper before handing the fish to hungry customers, and other salesmen hawked their wares. Samantha wondered why Johnny had chosen this route rather than taking Commerce where the traffic flowed without distraction. She was just about to ask him when he pulled his roadster to a stop along the curb. "Just running for some smokes," he said as he climbed out. "Be a minute."

Samantha fumed at being left to wait while Johnny ran a personal errand. She wasn't his girlfriend, she was his co-worker, and her time was just as valuable as his. She was working out in her mind how she was going to pull a strip off him when she caught a glimpse of a familiar form browsing the markets. It was Madame Mercier. Samantha lowered her sunglasses and watched the woman from over the top of the rims. She wouldn't have thought that the brothel mistress would do her own shopping. The madam held up an apple at the fruit stall and made a show of examining it before handing the vendor a coin.

Just then a car approached, slowing as it passed Samantha, but driving by without seeing her there. Samantha was shocked to see that it was Bobby Ryan whom they'd just left at the wharf. What was he doing here?

She chided herself. Probably just looking for a bit of lunch. His car slowed to a stop right in front of the fruit stall. His windows were already down, and he stuck his head out and whistled. Madame Mercier turned. Was Bobby Ryan actually soliciting the madam in broad daylight?

The fun didn't end there. Madame Mercier sauntered over to Bobby Ryan, casually yet somehow sensually biting into her apple. She leaned into his window, and they started chatting.

What Samantha wouldn't have given to be able to read lips! Had Bobby arranged to meet with her earlier? Was he reporting to her about being questioned at the wharf? Samantha's gut was telling her that these two were somehow involved—the question was how?

Their conversation was short, and Madame Mercier smiled and wiggled her fingers as she walked away in the direction of 29 Endicott Street. Bobby Ryan took off.

A second later, Johnny jumped into the car. Samantha had all but forgotten about her indignation and immediately told Johnny what he'd missed.

He spoke with a freshly lit cigarette hanging from

his lips. "Probably just a coincidence." He smirked. "My bet is Bobby Ryan has enjoyed Madame Mercier's company before if you know what I mean."

"I know what you mean," she spat. "I'm not stupid. Or naïve."

"Okay. Calm down." Johnny pulled his car into traffic. "No need to be so sensitive."

Samantha huffed. Johnny could be such a cad. And darn it, he was probably right. She needed to hone her instincts if she wanted to succeed as an investigative reporter.

Johnny pulled up in front of the *Daily Record* and turned off the ignition.

"Hey, before we go inside," he said, "I gotta question."

Samantha eyed her co-worker suspiciously. "Ya?"

"Will you go out with me?"

Samantha jerked back. "What?"

"Go out with me. I know a place. A little dancing and a little 'fishing'. It'd be fun."

"You mean a Chinese Laundry?" Samantha knew about the illegal clubs allegedly tucked in around the city, but with Talia, she didn't get out much.

"Yeah. They're harmless. You'll have fun."

Why'd he have to ask her out? He knew she'd say no. She shook her head.

"Oh, come on. I'm not asking you to marry me," he added slyly. "I know someone else has got that base covered." Johnny was like a dog with a bone when he wanted something, but she had to give him credit for not exposing her secret these last five years.

He continued. "You're too serious, Sam. Come out and take the edge off. It'll make you a better reporter, I tell you."

Samantha was about to politely decline until he added that last sentence.

"How so?"

"How so, what?"

"How will it make me a better reporter?"

"Oh, that's easy. It's a who-you-know world, doll. The more contacts you make, the more information comes your way. And you need that to write a good story."

Johnny made a good argument. Samantha wanted to write a good story. Not just a *good* story, but the *best* story.

"Okay."

Johnny laughed. "Hot dog! It's a date."

Samantha protested. "It's not a *date*!"

9

—————

*U*nlike the majority of the Italian community who lived in near-poverty conditions, the Marchesi family resided in a rare single-family home of mansion proportions. Having worked six years for the Massachusetts General Hospital, Haley had grown very familiar with all the city's neighborhoods and specifically where Boston's prestigious first families (such as the Lowells and Cabots) lived, and the wealthy Mob and Mafia families.

As Haley made her way to the front door, she had a fleeting thought that Detective Cluney would most certainly disapprove, and strongly at that, if he knew she was investigating this case on her own. It wasn't her job. It was dangerous. She could compromise the police investigation.

She knew all this was true, and still she lifted and

dropped the brass knocker lion attached to the center of the door.

Why was she doing it? Haley supposed a doctor of psychiatry would theorize that deep in her subconscious she was frustrated that neither she nor the police had found Joseph's killer. Haley didn't think one needed a doctorate to theorize that. Since her return to Boston, something *had* driven her to solve murder cases, and in all likelihood, it was that. She was frustrated. It was a pain that burned deep in her soul which only found a bit of respite when she successfully solved, or helped to solve, a case.

The respite was temporary, of course. Like a drug addict, the euphoria only lasted so long, and she needed to find another injection. Or the next case, as it were.

A slender maid answered the door wearing a black dress and a typical white cap and apron.

"Yes?" she asked cautiously.

"My name is Dr. Haley Higgins. I'm the assistant to the chief medical examiner. My condolences on the death of Mr. Stefano Marchesi."

The maid blanched and stepped outside into the brisk air, closing the door until it was only opened a crack.

With a strong Italian accent, she said, "Ve don't speak about Mr. Stefano here, Dr. Higgins. It vill be best if you vent avay immediately."

LEE STRAUSS

"Perhaps there is a member of the family who wouldn't mind talking with me?"

As if on cue, the door flew open, and a strong male form, probably in his mid-thirties, filled the space.

"Maria?" The man spoke in perfect English. "What's going on?"

"I'm sorry, Mr. Marchesi," the maid said. "We've got company."

The man's gaze washed over Haley, and his expression changed in a manner she had become accustomed to when assessed by the opposite sex. Curious interest, to disappointment, to dismissal. Haley lifted her square chin defiantly. She knew she wasn't the most beautiful of women, nor the most fashionable, but she was neatly put together in her summer dress suit and straw hat.

"I'm Dr. Haley Higgins, assistant to the medical examiner. Could you spare a few moments to chat?"

Mr. Marchesi might have been part of a Mob family, but he did prove to have manners. "Do come in, Doctor, before you catch a chill."

Inside, the man instructed the maid to bring coffee, and then he led Haley to a sitting room that might've taken her breath away if she hadn't had opportunity in the past to associate with the upper classes. Many valuable paintings hung on the richly papered walls. Haley recognized some of them as Van Gogh and Virgilio Tojetti. Surely they weren't originals, but even limited prints would cost a pretty penny. The furnishings were luxurious with the latest in interior design fashions, primarily of jade velour and ornate wooden trim. A large chandelier hung from the ceiling.

"I'm afraid I failed to introduce myself." Mr. Marchesi extended his right arm. "I'm Edoardo Marchesi."

With her gloves remaining on, Haley accepted the man's handshake. "Thank you for seeing me." She took the proffered seat.

"I'm assuming you're here because you have questions about my brother's death."

"Yes. That's correct."

"And you're working with the police?"

Haley ducked her chin in a nod as if not saying the word minimized the lie.

"I performed your brother's autopsy."

"Is that so? Forgive me for saying, but your profession doesn't appear very ladylike."

"Science has no gender, Mr. Marchesi."

His dark eyes flashed with amusement. "Very well. What are your questions?"

Before Haley could ask the first one, the maid, Maria, entered with a tray holding a French press—the glass carafe had loose grounds pressed to the bottom with a mesh plunger—, and two tiny porcelain cups. There was no cream on offer, only sugar. Haley didn't mind. She appreciated a strong cup of coffee, and honestly, she could use a little boost.

After a sip, she said, "I understand that your brother was estranged from the family."

Edoardo snorted. "You do cut to the chase, don't you, Dr. Higgins."

"I believe it's worthwhile to get the obvious out of the way."

Edoardo's full lips broke into a smile. "You're very intriguing, Doctor. Not at all what I expected you to be when I invited you in."

Haley didn't bite. Perhaps he thought, based on her looks and dress, that she'd be dull. A stereotypic school-marm. She asked again, "Why were you and your brother estranged?"

Edoardo sipped his coffee and then stared at her over the rim. "Not that it's any of your business, and I'm sure the police already know, but Stefano broke rule *numero uno*—don't play in your brother's sand-box." He smirked. "In other words, he slept with my wife."

"Oh." Haley wasn't shocked by much, but Mr. Marchesi's candidness caught her off guard.

Edoardo placed his coffee on the end table and leaned forward, placing his elbows on his knees. "You're not working with the police, are you, Dr. Higgins? So tell me, why are you really here?"

"I'm here out of curiosity."

Edoardo leaned back in his chair, his gaze never leaving hers, and smiled crookedly. "Curiosity killed the cat, Doctor. If I were you, I'd attend to my own business."

It was a warning. Haley, dismayed, felt her cheeks

heat up.

Standing, she said, "I'm sure you're right. Thank you once again for your time. I can find my way out."

LATER THAT AFTERNOON, Samantha pushed her daughter on a swing in a nearby park. Not so much a park as an empty lot, with a tree, and a tire hanging by a thick rope. Kids often fought over the right to ride it, but today, Samantha and Talia were fortunate enough to be alone, probably because all the other kids were in their homes eating supper. She and Talia had eaten earlier, and Samantha was keen to get some time alone with her daughter, out of the way of Bina's intrusive eyes. Besides, something troubled Samantha.

"Talia," she began, letting the tire swing slowly. "Are you really getting teased at school?"

Talia let the toes of her shoes drag through a dusty hole that had formed underneath by all the other hundreds of shoes that had done the same thing.

She answered softly, "Sometimes."

"What do the kids say?"

"I dunno."

Samantha squatted until she was eye-level with her daughter. "Don't be embarrassed. There's nothing, *nothing* you can't tell me. I'm always here for you."

Talia's lips began to tremble. "They're just so mean, Mommy. They call me names because I'm

Jewish, even though I tell them I'm only *half* Jewish. The boys push me around."

The injustice inflicted on her child burned in Samantha's chest. "They're just ignorant and bigoted."

"I don't know what that means."

"It means they're not worth a second thought or another tear. The next time they say something unkind, you say, racism is for simpletons.

"Racism is for simpletons," Talia repeated. "I don't know what that means either."

"Neither will they, but it'll shut them up."

At least, Samantha hoped it would. "Come, let's go see what Bina has baked today."

Talia wiped her nose with the back of her bare arm, and then took Samantha's hand.

Samantha wondered if Bina was right. Maybe a Jewish school would be best for Talia. It wouldn't prevent the rest of the city, or the rest of the world for that matter, from striking their punches, but at least she wouldn't get bullied there. At least not for being Jewish.

"Mommy?"

"Honeybun?"

"Why don't I have a daddy? Other kids have a daddy. Why don't I?"

Samantha sighed. It seemed that Talia was intent on crushing her mama's heart, pouring out all her problems in one go. Talia hadn't even been born yet when Seth left. Samantha had been naïve when she thought she could forget the grifter and move on. Even in his absence, her no-good husband proved to be a pain in the neck.

"You do have a daddy," Samantha said. "He's just not here, with us."

Talia tilted her head back to look up and almost lost her straw hat.

Samantha caught it before it fell into the dirt.

With her small voice, Talia asked, "Where is he, then?"

"I don't know, honey. He's lost."

"Then we need to go find him."

Samantha stared down at Talia's large, hopeful eyes. She shook her head. "Oh, honey. I'm afraid that some people just can't be found."

10

*W*henever Haley had a day off, at least in the summer months, she drove to the Country Golf Club in Brookline. Today was no different, and with her clubs in the backseat of the DeSoto, and the windows wide open, Haley motored southeast. The warm summer wind blew her curls loose from their pins, but she didn't mind. There was something soothing about letting convention go once in a while. A pair of round-frame sunglasses propped on her nose reduced the glare of the rising sun.

She eventually hit Clyde Street and parked in the lot in front of the clubhouse, a large, impressive three-story building that had a wall of windows and gabled wings on either end.

Haley wrestled her curls back into submission, donned her wide-brimmed hat, and hoisted her clubs from the backseat.

Inside the brightly painted lobby, Haley removed her sunglasses and registered to play. Members milled about and Haley was shocked to catch the eye of Mr. Edoardo Marchesi. The fact that he would be a member wasn't too surprising—since 1929, membership had fallen and only those with comfortable financial resources could continue to play. The Marchesi family certainly qualified. Only, Haley had never seen Edoardo Marchesi here before, or perhaps, she'd never registered his presence before, but somehow she doubted she'd miss noticing such a suave and charismatic man.

More shockingly, he approached her.

"Dr. Higgins," he said with a tip of his hat. "What a pleasant surprise."

Haley couldn't tell if he was being sincere or facetious. Considering he'd practically thrown her out of his house the one and only time they'd met, she leaned toward the latter.

She responded, "Indeed."

"Are you playing alone?"

"I am." Haley boldly looked the handsome man in the eyes. "I'm quite competitive with myself. I like to see if I can beat my last performance."

"I admire your individuality."

Again, Haley couldn't tell if the man was genuine in his praise, or concealing mockery.

"Thank you," Haley replied, simply. "Please excuse me. I like to complete the course before noon."

"Of course. Might I suggest we play together? I can be quite competitive as well, and I'm sure you'd enjoy the challenge."

Stunned by the proposal, Haley tightened her jaw before it could drop open.

"Surely, you came with companions who'd expect you to play with them?"

Edoardo Marchesi glanced at a group of men hovering to one side, and then dipped his chin. It was some kind of message, because the men immediately retreated. He turned back to Haley. "In fact, I'm alone. You won't refuse me a game, will you?"

Haley fumed. She couldn't very well be rude to the man, especially since other members had overheard this part of their conversation and were casting furtive glances their way.

Without smiling, Haley said, "I accept your challenge. But I only have time for nine holes." She put her sunglasses on and walked purposefully toward the exit.

Edoardo kept pace with her and opened the door in a gentlemanly gesture. Once outside, he motioned for a couple of caddies to assist, and within moments, Haley was relieved of her clubs.

They headed to the first hole in silence. Normally, the hike to the first hole brought Haley a sense of stress release, but this time her shoulders remained tight. Her mind worked quickly: why had Edoardo Marchesi latched on to her? Did he think she'd discovered evidence against him regarding the murder of his brother? Was he about to ply her with probing questions?

Was she in danger?

A man of Edoardo's stature and strength could easily overpower her. A person could meander about the course for a length of time without seeing another golfer.

She looked appreciatively at the two caddies, grateful for their company.

When they reached the hole, Edoardo said, "Ladies first."

Haley set a ball on the tee and requested a club. The lush green of the course spread out before her, with sandpits on either side of the hole. Groves of oak trees dotted the edges, their leaves blowing gently in the breeze.

Haley took her position, legs spread slightly, shoulders square, and swung. The ball lifted into the air, arched and landed a few feet from the hole.

Edoardo grinned. "Impressive, Dr. Higgins."

Haley accepted the accolade, and stepped back for Edoardo.

He repeated Haley's performance with his ball landing just shy of the hole. Haley blinked. That was darned near a hole-in-one!

"I'm the one who's impressed," she said.

They walked across the greens, caddies a discreet distance behind them, without a word. Haley considered her situation. She had the next shot, but if she missed, Edoardo was certain to get his.

She couldn't miss.

And she didn't! She barely held in a smirk.

"You're a worthy competitor," Edoardo said. He made his shot easily.

As they walked to the next hole, Haley said, "So why are you really playing golf with me?" She knew it wasn't due to physical attraction. He'd made that clear at their first encounter.

"I simply want to play with someone who could possibly beat me."

"And I'm that person? How would you know?"

"I asked at the desk."

Haley shot him a look. Was he telling the truth?

Another option made her blood grow cool. Had he followed her here?

Their competitive spirits came to the forefront on the next hole. Haley got it in two, Edoardo in three. Edoardo whistled in admiration. Haley bit her lip to keep from grinning. Good sportsmanship demanded it.

"Your perception of my motives was correct," Edoardo admitted, as they strolled past a sandpit and toward the next hole. "I did want to talk to you about something other than your golf game."

"Stefano?"

"Yes."

She'd been right. Edoardo thought she knew something and wanted to know what. "Okay," she said cautiously.

"I want to hire you to investigate his murder."

"What?" That was the last thing Haley had expected.

"I don't trust the cops, especially that half-wit, Cluney."

"I thought you had disowned your brother?"

"Stefano brought shame to my family, but he was still my brother. Whoever killed him should be hanged."

Haley inclined her head. "How do I know it wasn't you?"

"Why would I hire you if I was guilty?"

"Precisely to throw me off the scent."

"Ha. I knew you were clever. Very well, include me in your investigation, but I can assure you it'll be a waste of your time. And my money, I might add."

"I don't understand why you're requesting this of me. You were quite adamant when I came to your house, that I stay out of your business."

"I had time to reconsider. And, I'll admit, I did a bit of research on you. You may not know this, but your reputation for assisting the police in closing difficult cases precedes you.

Haley said nothing as they strolled to the next hole. She was both flattered and disturbed by Edoardo Marchesi's revelation. Pleased that she was commended, distressed that a Mafia man had been looking into her business and private life.

They completed the next hole before she responded.

"I'm not a private detective, Mr. Marchesi. Despite the fact that I often work with the police department, there must be someone you know who's more qualified than I."

"As you must be aware, I'm rather well known in Boston. I don't want everyone to know my business. You're a doctor, therefore you know what confidentiality entails. And you're just as intelligent as any of those gumshoes."

"I need time to think about it," Haley said.

Edoardo grinned. "You have five more holes."

They played the rest of the game as if golf was the only thing on their minds. Was she really going to consider working for the Mafia? No. Her answer must be no.

They ended nine holes with a matching score.

"You continue to surprise me, Dr. Higgins. I've never played with a lady who could keep up before."

"Thank you," Haley said. This time she couldn't keep the smile from tickling her lips.

"And do I have an answer?" Edoardo asked.

"I don't—"

He cut her off before she could finish.

"You're not about to back down from a challenge, are you, Dr. Higgins?"

Haley swallowed. "I'm not afraid of the challenge, I'm just—"

"Do you think you'll fail?"

"I'm not saying that!"

"You will work for me, then?"

Before she could check herself, the words left her mouth. "I will."

11

---

*O*h dear. Haley nibbled her lips as she drove back to the north end. What had she just agreed to? Joining forces with a Mafia family? Her competitive nature had really gotten her into trouble this time!

The only thing she could do now was to solve the case, give credit to the police department, and stay far away from Edoardo Marchesi.

And under no circumstances could she allow him to compensate her.

Besides, she wasn't convinced that he hadn't pulled the trigger himself. His ego was large enough that he'd think himself invincible. He was probably playing her like a fiddle for his own amusement.

The thought infuriated her and she blew loudly through her lips at the stray curl that had fallen into her eyes.

She pulled abruptly into a spot in front of her apartment building, hoisted the leather bag of clubs onto her back, and, despite the extra weight, practically sprinted up the stairs, fueled as she was by her eagerness to get to work on this case.

Molly greeted her at the door. "Hello, Dr. Higgins. How was golf this morning?"

Haley set her clubs down in the corner behind the door and removed her hat.

"I fear I've done something quite foolish, Molly."

"I highly doubt that," Molly said kindly. "You don't have a foolish bone in your body."

"I grew one today." Haley filled Molly in over a lunch of tuna sandwiches, fresh strawberries, and hot tea. She found a measure of peace in her confession. "The only thing I can do now is find the killer, and then never cross paths with Mr. Marchesi again."

"Yes, well, if anyone can, it's you," Molly said. "But do be careful. The Marchesis are dangerous bedfellows."

"I will." Haley rose from the table and took her dirty dishes to the sink. "Now, if you need me, I'll be in my office."

Sitting at her desk, Haley removed a pad of paper from the top drawer, opened it to a blank page, and selected a sharpened pencil.

What facts did she have so far? In smooth cursive she began to write:

- Stefano Marchesi - shot point blank from inside the Bell in Hand.
- Mike Tobin - possible witness, but denies seeing the shooter.
- The outside shooting spree a decoy. By whom? E. Marchesi's henchmen?
- Stefano Marchesi frequent customer of Madame Mercier's brothel. Death of Agnes O'Reilly, alias Snowflake, related somehow?

Haley chewed on the end of her pencil. Who were the viable suspects and what were the possible motives?

- Edoardo Marchesi - betrayal
- Mike Tobin – misunderstanding over contraband?
- One of the prostitutes? - Scorned lover?
- Another "fisherman"?

Haley realized with dismay that she hadn't even visited the victim's place of work. She really did have to raise the bar on her investigation if she was going to get to the bottom of this. Briefly, she thought about visiting Detective Cluney, but pushed the idea aside. He'd only chide her for getting in the way of police business—and rightly so. If he found out she'd agreed to work for

Edoardo Marchesi, the detective might just put her behind bars!

Gathering her purse, hat, and the keys to the DeSoto, Haley let Molly know she was leaving, and then headed to the docks.

A big steamship had recently docked and the number of men scurrying about could populate a small town. Crates were being unloaded by large cranes, then loaded into delivery trucks.

Obviously at the wrong wharf, Haley turned her DeSoto around in search of the fishing vessels. She hadn't had a reason to frequent the wharves, and found herself at a loss. Boston Harbor housed many docks, but she finally drove down one that looked promising. Silver-backed fish piled on the deck of a fishing boat shimmered in the glare of the sun.

In her haste, Haley had forgotten her sunglasses and she lowered the brim of her hat in an effort to cut the glare. Though clearly the only woman walking along the dock, her presence only triggered the odd cursory glance. She told herself it was because live fish needed to be moved on in a timely manner, but she couldn't help but wonder if Miss Hawke would've gotten more attention.

One man carried a square case off the boat— looking suspiciously like it contained bottles and nothing that resembled sea life. He startled when he noticed her, placed the box down on the dock, and stood in front of it.

"You must be lost," he said. He wore brown work pants held up by black suspenders. The sleeves of his dirty white shirt were rolled up as high as possible revealing strong arms. A flat cap sat on short, greasy hair. He was an average-looking fellow, except for the deformation of one ear, commonly known as cauliflower ear.

Haley pulled out a photograph of Stefano Marchesi's face she'd taken in the lab. "Do you recognize this man?"

He turned his head to his good ear, indicating that he was hard of hearing. "What's that?"

Haley repeated her question. Recognition flashed behind the man's eyes. "We already talked to the reporters." He retrieved his box and stepped around her. Haley followed with long strides. "Do you know him?"

"Everyone knows March. Idiot got himself killed."

"Did you work with him?"

"Like I said, everyone knew him. No one much cares that he's dead."

The man loaded his box into the back of a truck and drove away. Haley let out a frustrated breath. Other efforts to engage the workingman proved futile, and she had no choice but to admit defeat.

She wondered if Miss Hawke knew who the reporters were, and what, if anything, they'd learned.

On her way home Haley stopped at the Bell in Hand Tavern. She wasn't interested in what was going on inside, but rather out. The windows had been repaired and patrons were coming and going, business as usual. She hoped to find "Ol Oscar," as Mike Tobin had called the homeless man and, who was, potentially, the only witness to the killing. She walked up and down Union and Marshall, but failed to find a person who'd fit Oscar's description. Enquiring as to his whereabouts produced shrugs and no information.

Perhaps Detective Cluney's men had been able to track him down, but she failed to imagine a compelling reason to ask the detective that wouldn't arouse his ire, and she couldn't afford to get on his bad side.

12

___

*S*amantha took a taxi to Franklin Street and tipped the driver fifty cents. She smoothed out her sleeveless silk dress made of Monet-blue georgette crepe. It draped from the right shoulder to the left and finished with an ornate row of tiny vertical-set rhinestone buttons. The picot-edged tiers of the skirt fell in layers from the hips with the hem landing just below the knee. She knew from her work on the women's articles that the outfit was tired, on its way out of style: the waist a little too low and a little too loose, and the hem a little too high. She should've added a belt to cinch the waist, and maybe something sewn on as a fringe to give it more length—as women were known to do in these economically trying times. Samantha had written an article on tips for bringing a 1920's outfit into the new decade. But the club would be dimly lit and all the clientele on their way to tipsy, so she thought she'd be all right.

Johnny was waiting where he said he'd be, leaning up against a lamppost and smoking a cigarette. He dropped it to the ground and stepped on it when he spotted her.

"I was worried you were going to stand me up."

"I said I would come, didn't I?"

Truth was, Samantha almost had bailed on her co-worker. Bina had griped about how much time Samantha spent away from home. Samantha had argued back that Talia was sleeping anyway.

"What if I wasn't here to watch her all the time," Bina had said. "Then what would you do?"

"I suppose I'd have to pay someone to look after her," she'd snapped. "What would you do?"

They'd had a stare-down where Samantha pursed her lips and Bina narrowed her watery brown eyes. Her mother-in-law would be on the streets if it weren't for Samantha's job, a job that included Samantha being away from home all the time. Where was her beloved son, huh? Left them all to rot! Bina should be thankful.

As a child, Samantha had been taught manners and to respect her elders. She held her tongue.

Besides, it wasn't like she was meeting Johnny and sneaking into a club for the fun of it. It was to make *connections*, which in her line of work, proved to be very important.

Johnny offered his arm, and Samantha linked her elbow with his.

They came to a set of concrete steps that led to the basement of a three-story brownstone. Johnny knocked, and a small window opened. Samantha strained to hear what Johnny said to the set of dark eyes staring back.

The real McCoy.

It was a reference to Captain William Frederick McCoy, the famous, or some would say, infamous, Floridian rum runner.

Inside, they were hit by loud, live music, raucous laughter, and a mix of smells, not entirely pleasant. Heavy perfume and cologne mixed with cigarette and cigar smoke, a waft of alcohol, along with the tang of sweat.

The environment—rich with color, lights, and beautiful people—completely distracted Samantha from the smell, which in a short amount of time, had miraculously faded away.

The room was cavernous, without windows, but with plenty of soft electric lights. Tables encircled a dance floor, full of entwined couples moving to the beat of the live jazz band at the back of the room. The band members were the only black faces, and quite possibly the most talented. Samantha had never seen a live band like it. It was pure energy and quite contagious. She had the urge to drag Johnny to the floor and start swinging.

Samantha played it cool, though. She didn't want Johnny to guess that this was her first time at a speakeasy.

Johnny removed his blazer, took Samantha's shawl and disappeared with them, leaving Samantha standing alone. The dancers mesmerized her. Their feet floated and tapped along the floor, doing something like the foxtrot, but sped up to double speed.

A skimpily dressed woman with a tray of drinks paused as she passed Samantha, and looked pointedly at Samantha's empty hands.

"Drink? I got French champagne or if you're looking for something stronger, Canadian whiskey."

"Champagne, please." Samantha opened the small purse that hung over her shoulder by a thin gold chain, looking for the dollar the waitress requested.

"I'll get that," Johnny said, with a sudden reappearance. He held out a folded bill clutched between two fingers.

"Don't be silly," Samantha said.

Johnny insisted. "I don't bring a dame to a club and then make her pay."

Samantha smiled, not wanting to make a scene, and waited for the woman and her tray to move on. She spoke into Johnny's ear, loud enough so he could hear her over the band. "Remember, this is not a date. It's business!"

Johnny chuckled, grabbed her hand, and led her to a recently vacated table.

Samantha sipped the champagne and took a moment to savor the quality. It was the real thing! She noticed that there were eyes on her, from both the men and women in the room. Despite her subpar clothing, Samantha knew that men found her attractive, and that some women found her threatening—a fact Samantha couldn't control. Even so, she wasn't above using her feminine wiles to get what she wanted.

A tall man with dark hair and a handsome face watched from his position across the room. He leaned narrow hips against the bar and coddled a glass of amber liquid in one hand, but his dark eyes had settled on her. Samantha tipped her glass in his direction in acknowledgement.

Johnny's head turned sharply and followed her gaze. "Be careful, doll. That's Edoardo Marchesi."

"Marchesi? As in the Mob family?" Samantha leaned in closer. "Are you telling me that gorgeous man is Stephen March's brother?"

Johnny grimaced, most likely at the use of the adjective "gorgeous" concerning Edoardo Marchesi.

"Yes, and yes. He's dangerous, Sam."

"He's walking over here."

"If he asks you to dance, say no."

"Of course."

"Excuse me for interrupting." Edoardo's voice was smooth as silk and refined like an educated man's. If Samantha hadn't known better, she'd never have guessed that the man wearing an expensive and well-fitted pinstriped suit was related to the man who'd worked on the wharf.

"I couldn't help but notice you as you walked in. Could I buy you a drink?"

Samantha nodded at her half-filled flute, though she doubted he hadn't seen her sip from it.

Johnny cleared his throat loudly. "I believe the lady is with me."

"I'm sorry," Edoardo said, not taking his eyes off Samantha. "I hadn't guessed that by the lady's behavior."

"My glass is still full," Samantha said with a smile.

"Perhaps I could interest you in a dance."

"I have two left feet."

"Perfect. I also have two left feet."

Edoardo Marchesi held out a hand, and Samantha found she couldn't resist taking it. Sure, he was handsome and debonair, but this was part of her *job*. She'd said yes out of *duty*.

The band played *Body and Soul*, a waltz that brought couples close. Holding Edoardo's hand and with her other palm on his shoulder, she found his nearness intoxicating. How long *had* it been?

She chided herself. *Stay professional!*

It turned out that Edoardo Marchesi had undersold his dancing abilities, and Samantha had as well.

"Now that we are properly acquainted," he said, "perhaps an introduction is in order. "I'm Edoardo Marchesi."

"I'm Samantha Ro-"

Samantha caught herself in time. She couldn't believe she'd almost said Rosenbaum! She did that sometimes when she was nervous. "Hawke," she added quickly.

"It's a pleasure, Miss Hawke."

"So, Mr. Marchesi?" she returned playfully. "I thought your work would keep you too busy for leisure pleasures such as this."

"Man cannot live by bread alone," he said, quoting Jesus. "Besides, I own this place."

"Really?" Samantha wondered if Johnny had known this all along. Was that why he'd chosen this speakeasy? A glance in his direction confirmed that he hadn't planned for this dance to happen. The scowl on his face was deeply grooved.

Edoardo commanded her gaze, and she gave it to him. "Why have I not seen you before?" he asked.

"Honestly? This is my first time. I'm a law-abiding citizen for the most part."

"What changed tonight?"

Samantha risked another glance at Johnny. He was conferring with another gentleman Samantha didn't recognize. The man was average height, muscular, with dirty-blond hair greased straight back from his forehead. He wore an ordinary blue suit.

She batted her eyelashes as she answered, "I got lonely."

Edoardo's grin widened. "Maybe I could help you out with that."

A cool thread of fear trickled down her spine. She was out of practice with men and had clearly sent the wrong signal.

"I'm not—"

They were interrupted by the man in the blue suit, the one who'd been in conference with Johnny.

"Might I cut in?"

Edoardo looked less than pleased, but Samantha grabbed on to the lifeline.

"Sure," Samantha said. To Edoardo, she added, "You don't mind, Mr. Marchesi, do you?" She smiled her most charming smile.

He bobbed his head. "Of course not. Until we meet again, Miss Hawke."

Johnny's acquaintance offered his hand, and Samantha took it.

"I'm assuming you know who I am," Samantha said politely. "Who are you?"

"The name's Bell. Tom Bell."

"And how do you know Mr. Milwaukee?"

"We have a friend in common."

"I see. Well, I didn't need rescuing." Despite the relief Samantha had originally felt, she would like to have thought she'd been capable of handling the situation on her own.

The song ended after a short turn, and Samantha

made it clear there'd not be a second song. "Thank you, Mr. Bell. My feet are tired, and I'm thirsty."

"Very well, Miss Hawke. Now don't be mad at Johnny. He was only concerned for your safety."

Samantha snorted as delicately as a lady might. Mr. Bell soon disappeared into the crowd.

"I can't believe you said yes," Johnny scolded. "You promised you'd say no to his offer."

"I promised no such thing," Samantha returned. "It was an opportunity to investigate. I should think you'd be glad."

"You're a wo—"

Samantha put up a palm. "Stop, Mr. Milwaukee, before you say something you'll regret."

13

The next morning, Haley stood in Dr. Guthrie's office with her arms folded. Though she could see through the glass wall that separated his office from the rest of the morgue, he also had a thorough view of Haley's workspace, including her desk in the opposite corner. She couldn't ignore him when he called her over.

She was stunned by his announcement. "Are you saying that the Marchesi family refuses to claim the body?"

Dr. Guthrie adjusted his glasses. "That's what I said, didn't I? You're not hard of hearing, are you?"

Haley narrowed her gaze disapprovingly. If there was a person in the room who was hearing-impaired, it certainly wasn't her. She ignored his jibe and plowed on. "It's bad enough that they created their wealth on the backs of the citizens of Boston, now they expect the taxpayers to pick up the tab to bury one of their own."

Stefano Marchesi wasn't the only one abandoned and scheduled for a pauper's field burial. Agnes O'Reilly's family were farmers in Ohio and couldn't afford to make a claim. They'd wondered if the rich family where their dear daughter, Agnes, had been employed would show mercy. Haley hadn't had the heart to tell Mr. O'Reilly the truth, and she doubted Madame Mercier would pay the fee for a proper burial. It didn't hurt to ask, Haley supposed.

Leaving Dr. Guthrie to "work" at his desk—meaning he'd be snoozing within ten minutes—Haley returned to her own to catch up on paperwork. Her mind went back to the death of Agnes O'Reilly, also known as Snowflake, and she mentally reviewed the scene of the crime. Her subconscious niggled. Something was amiss. If only she could see those photographs Miss Hawke had taken.

It wasn't a big surprise that Miss Hawke had failed her. Members of the press were like vultures, circling the carcass, looking for a bit of meat they could snag. They weren't interested in sharing, and they didn't care if they had to fight one another and squawk loudly to get what they wanted.

Haley had hoped Miss Hawke was different.

Then again, Miss Hawke had kept her promise so far and hadn't published the story. And the photographs hadn't shown up anywhere yet. Maybe

Miss Hawke hadn't had a chance to develop them. Or worse, she'd bungled the process, and Haley could never hope to see them.

Yesterday, she had tried her luck at investigating Mr. March's death, to no avail. Maybe she'd have better odds with Miss O'Reilly. Haley opened the girl's file and read her notes again.

Twenty-year-old Caucasian female of Irish descent. Five foot four, one hundred and twelve pounds. First-trimester pregnancy. Cause of death: gunshot to the frontal lobe.

Just when Haley was about to give up and make herself a coffee, someone knocked on the door. She could've called out for the person to come in, but she'd been sitting for a while and getting to her feet would do her good. She opened the door and was speechless. Standing before her was Miss Hawke.

"Dr. Higgins, I hope I'm not interrupting."

"Not at all," Haley said. "I was just thinking about you."

Miss Hawke waved a manila envelope. "You were wondering about these, I bet."

"Indeed, I was."

Samantha Hawke held out the envelope, and Haley happily received it. She waited for the reporter to leave, yet Miss Hawke remained with a look of expectation.

"Is there something else, Miss Hawke?"

"I was hoping you'd allow me to look over them with you. I've studied them myself, you see."

"And found nothing of use?"

"Well, not really. But you have a trained eye. Would you allow me to stay? Please?"

Haley let out a short breath. It would be rude to refuse Miss Hawke's request, especially since she'd taken and developed the photographs at Haley's prompting.

"Certainly. I was about to make coffee. Would you like some?"

"I would. Thank you."

Haley directed Miss Hawke to an empty chair then proceeded to make the coffee with her French press. Haley didn't mind the silence between them, she was used to a quiet room, but it seemed that Miss Hawke felt it necessary to fill it.

"I've never been inside a morgue before," she said. "I thought it would be darker and dreary. Sinister even."

"It's a common misconception," Haley replied.

"Do you like your job? You know, dealing with death all the time? You don't find it depressing?"

"I'm a scientist. I like to use my skills to speak for the dead. I consider myself their advocate."

"That's very noble of you."

Haley shot Miss Hawke a look. Was she being smart? No, she didn't appear to be.

"I'm no different than any other doctor."

When the coffee was ready, Haley poured two cups. "Milk and sugar?"

"Yes, please."

"What about you, Miss Hawke?" Haley said once she had positioned herself behind her desk. "What is it about working for a newspaper that interests you?"

"Well, I suppose I like that I'm involved with keeping people informed. I normally write the women's pages. I recently have been assigned a criminal case."

"Miss O'Reilly's?"

"No. Mr. Marchesi."

"Ah. It appears that no one is interested in Miss O'Reilly."

"I am."

Haley lowered her cup and studied her guest. Haley was acquainted with a lot of attractive women and didn't hold it against them. They were no more at fault for being pretty than she was for being plain. It was only a problem for Haley when a lady who was so gifted wore it as if it was a badge of honor, and not something unearned.

Samantha Hawke wasn't like that.

"Is that why you want to study the photographs with me. To solve the case?"

Miss Hawke nodded.

"And not just to get a story?"

"You won't penalize me for wanting both, Dr. Higgins, will you? I'm afraid I can't have one without the other. You see, it's not only me I have to think about. I have dependents."

Miss Hawke didn't elaborate, and Haley thought it improper to probe. That didn't mean she wasn't curious. Perhaps she had a pile of younger siblings to help feed. It was a common enough situation.

"Very well," Haley said, standing. With the envelope in hand, she moved to a bare table and removed the photographs. She arranged the pictures in the order she remembered having Miss Hawke take them.

With a nod of her head, she indicated that her guest could join her. "Let's have a look at these then, shall we?"

THERE HAD BEEN a brief moment when Samantha thought this serious woman was going to toss her out of the morgue. Dr. Higgins was a brilliant scientist, but despite her no-nonsense presentation, Samantha saw depths of feeling in the doctor's chestnut-brown eyes. Empathy, that was what it was. Despite their differences in appearance and occupation, Sam realized that she and Dr. Higgins had more in common than not.

If only the good doctor would come to the same conclusion. A slim possibility hung in the air that perhaps the two of them could become friends.

Or at least friendly.

Dr. Higgins had wild, curly hair, barely tamed by

the pins that sought to rule and maintain order, and more than once she pushed a wayward strand behind her ear as she stared through a large magnifying glass.

"What do you see?" Samantha asked. She, too, had spent a good amount of time staring at the photographs through an eyepiece and had concluded nothing.

Dr. Higgins didn't answer, just moved around the table as she examined each photo, muttering to herself as she reviewed the crime scene.

"This is from the door. This one from the foot of the bed. And from the window." Dr. Higgins scoured a close-up of the victim.

"What do you see?" Samantha said again, failing to keep her voice from sounding too eager.

"A dead woman."

Samantha snorted. "Very funny. There's obviously something there or did I waste my time? Oh, and money, I might add."

"Yes."

"Yes, what? There's something there, or I wasted my time."

"One of the two."

"Dr. Higgins!"

The doctor looked up as if she were surprised that Samantha was still there.

"I'm sorry. I feel like I'm missing something. Forgive my shortness."

"Do you feel it in your gut?" Samantha asked. She

pressed a fist against her stomach. "I do. I feel it right here. We're missing something."

Dr. Higgins' gaze dropped to the fist pressing against Samantha's stomach and then back at the photographs."

"That's it," she said.

"What's it?" Samantha asked. "What's *it?*"

Samantha watched as Dr. Higgins gathered the photographs, slid them into the envelope, stepped quickly to her desk, and put them in the top drawer. She then collected her hat and summer crocheted gloves, poked her head into the neighboring office, and startled the older man sitting there. Samantha didn't even realize they hadn't been alone all this time.

"I'm going out," Dr. Higgins announced.

"Yes, yes," the man said, then lowered his chin and closed his eyes.

The doctor stared at Samantha. "Are you coming?

14

Samantha was a little annoyed that Dr. Higgins refused to say more about what she thought she saw in the photographs.

"It's just a theory," Dr. Higgins explained as they drove together in the doctor's DeSoto.

Samantha sensed the wall of distrust Dr. Higgins had put up between them. She supposed it was something she needed to get used to if she wanted to pursue investigative journalism. In that regard, writing for the women's pages was different. The ladies behind the perfume counter at Sears never watched her with suspicion and were more than pleased to be getting free advertising.

Now she stood beside Dr. Higgins on the stoop of Madame Mercier's place of business. It was the first time Samantha had noticed Dr. Higgins' height. With the lower military heel of her buckled-up Oxford pumps, Dr. Higgins had to be close to six feet tall.

The door was opened quickly when Dr. Higgins knocked.

A girl with a flushed face wearing a scandalously short housedress blurted, "Are you the midwife?"

Samantha shared a quick look with Dr. Higgins. As far as she could tell, their decision to visit the brothel had been unannounced. "She's upstairs. It's bad."

A loud wail erupted from the upper floor, and Dr. Higgins broke into a run. Samantha sprinted after her.

A stern-faced Madame Mercier stood in the hall-way. "It's not you I called."

"As it happens, I'm here," Dr. Higgins said. "Can I assume that a lady present is in labor?"

Madame Mercier shrugged a bare shoulder.

"Then allow me to assist until the midwife you've summoned has arrived."

"Very well. Her name is Primrose."

When they were led to the room where Agnes O'Reilly had died, Samantha raised a brow in question.

"No one vants to use zees room for entertaining anymore," Madame Mercier explained.

The mother-to-be was in bad shape. Her skin glistened with sweat, her hair was matted, and her clothing was nearly transparent from the heat of her exertion.

"Oh, no!" she cried as another labor pain began.

"How long has she been laboring?" Dr. Higgins asked.

"Since yesterday," Madame Mercier replied.

The doctor's dark brows shot up, and Samantha shared her questioning look.

Dr. Higgins moved to the bedside. "Why has the midwife not been called before now?"

Madame Mercier's lips pulled down. "First babies always take their sweet time. Zee midwife charges by zee hour."

Primrose let out another yelp as a new labor pain took hold. Samantha watched with sympathy, having gone through the experience once herself.

Dr. Higgins took charge. "Get me some clean towels, and a pitcher of boiled water." The girl who'd opened the front door for them hurried away.

Dr. Higgins took Primrose's hand and smiled down at her. "Hello, Primrose. I'm Dr. Higgins. I'm here to help."

The poor girl burst into tears. "I'm so scared. And so, so tired."

"Well, try to sleep a bit in between contractions."

"Thank you." The words were barely audible. Primrose closed her eyes, and it appeared to Samantha that she'd fallen asleep.

Dr. Higgins gently pressed her fingers along the woman's protruding belly. Her expression tightened in concern.

"What is it?" Samantha asked.

Dr. Higgins spoke through tight lips. "Breech."

Samantha understood the seriousness of that. The baby was bottom first, and a natural delivery would be very difficult. "Can you turn it around?"

"It might just turn on its own. I've seen it happen."

"Have you delivered many babies before?" Samantha asked. This wasn't something she'd thought a doctor of pathology would tend to do.

"I worked on several hospital wards as an intern, including maternity, before I decided on my major."

Primrose gasped awake as the next contraction took hold.

Samantha wondered what would happen to the baby when it came. A child on the premises would surely be bad for Madame Mercier's business, and Samantha couldn't imagine the brothel mistress permitting it. If the mother kept the child, they were sure to be impoverished. Samantha sighed. There'd be no happy ending here.

Primrose collapsed back onto her pillow. Her skin was a disturbing shade of white, almost blue, and she was drenched with sweat. Dr. Higgins patted her patient's face with a damp cloth. She took hold of Primrose's wrist with two fingers, and Samantha watched as the doctor counted.

"It's very low."

While Dr. Higgins sat with her patient, Samantha took turns pacing and sitting in the wooden chair in the corner of the room. She wondered why she stayed. It wasn't as if she were of any practical help, but she felt she could offer moral support. And she did want to see the baby born safely. For some reason, witnessing that was important to her.

Samantha spoke to Madame Mercier asking for cups of coffee, a request the woman reluctantly conceded to. "Ve're not a restaurant."

One of the girls brought a tray with the coffee.

"Milk and sugar?" Samantha said.

Dr. Higgins nodded. "Please."

Samantha prepared a mug and handed it to the doctor. "How is she doing?"

"Poor thing's completely worn out, and her blood pressure is so low." She turned away from the woman in the bed and lowered her voice. "I don't know if she can do this."

Suddenly, Primrose sprung up as another strong labor pain began. She let out a guttural cry as she pushed.

"It's coming," Dr. Higgins said.

Samantha's heart raced. "Did it turn?"

"No. It's coming bottom first."

Samantha felt faint as she witnessed the new mother's agony. Memories of her own experience giving birth returned with a vengeance. Hers had been painful but quick, and her recovery short. Samantha was one of the fortunate ones.

"One more push, Primrose!" Dr. Higgins said.

"I can't! I'm so tired."

"You must."

Another strong contraction forced the matter, and a tiny, slippery baby landed in Dr. Higgins' arms.

Samantha let out a breath of relief as a sense of awe at the miracle of birth flooded her. A tiny, perfectly formed human being let out a soft cry.

"You did it, Primrose," Dr. Higgins said. "You have a son." She wiped the babe down with a damp cloth then wrapped him in a towel. Primrose had collapsed on the large pillow behind her. Pale and drawn, the woman looked frail and completely exhausted.

Samantha jerked in surprise when Dr. Higgins offered the baby to her.

"Please hold him," she said. "The placenta is coming next."

Samantha received the snugly swaddled child and stared at his perfectly formed face. "Hi, little man. Welcome to the world."

Suddenly, a flash flood of blood turned the white sheets bright crimson.

"I need those towels!" Dr. Higgins said.

With the tiny baby cradled in one arm, Samantha hurried to grab the stack of towels on the opposite end table. It was obvious by the amount of blood that Primrose was hemorrhaging.

Samantha watched in horror as Dr. Higgins struggled to stop the flow of blood, but there was no resisting Mother Nature.

"Can you save her?"

Dr. Higgins took Primrose's pulse, then stared back at Samantha with sorrow in her eyes. She pushed back dark curls from her weary-looking face. "I'm afraid she's already dead."

15

*H*aley had brought unusual things home to Molly before—old bones, organs sealed in mason jars, miscellaneous objects of interest to science—but this was the first time she'd brought home a newborn.

Molly's round jaw slackened, and her mouth opened. "A baby?"

"He's a guest, Molly. Only temporary." Haley lowered the baby basket onto the kitchen table along with a canvas bag containing glass baby bottles, a stack of small diapers, plastic pants, diaper pins, and spit-up cloths she'd obtained from the hospital nursery. "His mother died during birth," Haley explained.

Molly made cooing sounds as she hovered over the child. "Oh, poor thing." She glanced up at Haley who was preparing a pot of water to heat on the stove. A bottle of formula bobbed about inside. "Let me do that," Molly insisted.

"I fed him at the hospital, but he's going to need feeding every three hours."

"The mite is on the small side, eh?" Molly said.

After a few minutes, Haley dripped a bit of formula onto her wrist to test the temperature. "This should do it." She held it out to Molly. "Would you like to do the honors?"

Molly's flushed face broke into a smile. "I sure would."

Molly settled in a rocking chair in the living room and teased the baby's lips with the rubber nub. Haley was pleased to see that he took it eagerly, a sign that he was in good health.

"Oh, aren't you as cute as a bug's ear," Molly cooed. "Aren't you?" To Haley, she said, "He's got a good appetite."

"Speaking of food," Haley said. "I'm starving."

"There's a ham and cheese sandwich in the refrigerator."

Haley retrieved the sandwich along with a glass of milk. She broke her own rule about eating in the living room and snuggled in beside the feline form curled up on the divan.

"Move over, Mr. Midnight."

"Does this baby have a name?" Molly asked.

"Not officially. The mother's name was Ellen

Proust." Haley had garnered this piece of information from Madame Mercier.

"We'll call him Master Proust then."

"Good idea."

"Is there a father?"

"Presumably, but no one seems to know who." In this case, Haley thought, it could be any of a number of men. "We'll try to locate the mother's family once we know who they are."

"I see," Molly said with understanding. The child was illegitimate and abandoned. She smiled softly at the baby. "He's fallen asleep."

Haley yawned. "I suppose we should sleep when he does. Shall we take turns feeding him overnight?"

"Not on your life," Molly said. "You have to work in the morning. Let me take care of little Master Proust."

"Are you sure?"

Molly seemed confident, but Haley had never seen her work with children or babies before. "Taking care of an infant is a lot of work."

Molly huffed. "I'm the oldest of nine. I practically raised my younger siblings."

"Very well, if you're sure. In the morning, I'm going to see about finding his family."

Molly's gaze moved to the clock sitting on the mantel over the fireplace. "Don't you have to go back to work?"

"I told Dr. Guthrie I was taking the rest of the day off."

"Good for you, Dr. Higgins. You work too hard."

It was Molly's usual complaint. Haley didn't have the heart to tell her she still meant to work that evening, just not at the morgue.

As serendipity would have it, Chantilly, wearing a thin shawl over bare shoulders, was approaching the door of Madame Mercier's house just as Haley pulled up. Haley honked, startling the poor girl.

She jumped out of the car and approached. "Hi Chantilly, sorry to scare you like that."

"I-it's fine." Chantilly had large hazel eyes and a small upturned nose. Her brunette hair was bobbed and pushed behind her ears. Her forehead was damp with perspiration.

"I was hoping we could talk," Haley said. "Could I buy you a coffee or some dinner?"

"I really should get inside."

"I'll talk to Madame Mercier if it makes a difference."

"No. You don't have to do that." Chantilly got into the car. "It's so nice of you to offer."

The Bell in Hand was only a few blocks away, and Haley thought she might kill two birds with one stone—question Chantilly about the brothel while keeping an eye on Mike Tobin and the happenings at the tavern.

Mr. Tobin scowled when he first saw Haley walk

in and did a double take when he saw who she was with.

"Do you two know each other?" Haley asked as they claimed a table.

Chantilly responded slyly. "We've met."

Haley wouldn't be surprised if Chantilly had *met* a lot of the men in the area.

Mr. Tobin forced a smile as he took their order.

"Those are straight coffees," Haley said with a look. She didn't think he'd bring whiskey in coffee cups, but she wanted to be sure.

Coffee was served along with the tuna sandwiches Haley had ordered, and Chantilly nearly inhaled hers. *Did Madame Mercier not feed her girls? They were rather thin, but that had been the style for a long time.* Haley hoped the fad to appear boyish was on its way out.

Once her appetite was satisfied, Chantilly said, "What did you want to ask me?"

"Do your visitors ever leave their shoes behind?"

"What?"

"I spotted a pair of men's shoes in the wardrobe." This was the fact that had niggled at Haley's subconscious. In the photograph, the heel of man's leather shoe could be seen through the crack of the wardrobe door that had hung ajar. "Is there ever a reason that a man would leave his shoes behind?"

Chantilly chuckled. "Not unless he was too drunk to notice he was in stocking feet."

Haley hummed. Maybe it was as simple as that, and she was making something out of nothing.

"Was that what you wanted to ask me?"

"Yes, but not all. I was hoping you could tell me a little more about Primrose."

Suspicion flashed behind Chantilly's eyes. "What do you want to know?"

"Is it possible that Snowflake knew who the father of Primrose's baby was?"

"Why do you want to know that?"

"Do *you* know who the father was?"

Chantilly crinkled her upturned nose. "I don't see why it's important."

"Maybe he wants the baby."

Chantilly scoffed. "Too late for that."

"Why?"

"Fine, I'll tell you, not that it's any business of yours."

Haley got the feeling Chantilly was dying for a bit of gossip. "Go on," she said, encouragingly.

"It was that March fellow."

Stunned, Haley stared back. "Stephen March?"

Chantilly's eyes twinkled. "He was killed here, wasn't he?" Her hand went to her mouth. "Don't tell me we're sitting at the very table!"

Thankfully, they were not. "No. He died further back in the room." Haley pressed on before Chantilly could take them off subject again. "So tell me, how could Primrose know for sure? Surely, there were other men—other possibilities."

Chantilly pushed her plate, which had barely a crumb remaining, to the side and sipped her coffee. "Mr. March was particular. He didn't like to share, you see. He paid extra for exclusive privileges."

Stefano Marchesi must've had access to some family money. Haley didn't think work on the wharfs paid that much. Of course, rum running could be lucrative.

"And Primrose was reserved for him?" Haley confirmed.

"That's right."

"Did he know the child was his?"

"Primrose's?"

"Who else?"

"Well, it was Snowflake that he loved. Or at least, that's what Snowflake said."

"Wait a minute; I'm confused. Stephen March was responsible for both? I thought Primrose was his exclusive."

"He was *her* exclusive. Didn't mean *he* had to be exclusive. Created a lot of tension between Primrose and Snowflake. They were good friends once. Both came from the same Midwestern town, forget now which one. Came to the city looking for work." She flicked a hand at herself. "Like a lot of girls, they ended up like this."

Haley sympathized.

Chantilly picked up on Haley's look. "But don't pity us. At least we have three meals a day and a roof over our heads. That's more than a lot of folks can say nowadays."

Haley conceded. America was in a depression, and life was hard for many.

"Why did Mr. March have to make use of Madame Mercier's business? Surely, a man at home with the ladies wouldn't have to pay for female company?"

"Snowflake said he didn't want a steady girl. Just the fun, ya know."

Haley was starting to form judgments against this guy. She shook her head to push the thoughts out. Sipping her coffee, she mused over this new information. Primrose had conceived first. If she had found out about Snowflake and Stephen March, maybe she'd become consumed with jealousy. It would be motive for murder. With Snowflake out of the way, Primrose might've hoped Mr. March would make her an honest woman and legitimize his child.

Her thoughts were brought back to the present by the sound of Chantilly's voice. "Besides, he was so charming, you couldn't help but fall in love with him just a little bit."

Haley considered Chantilly's statement, then asked. "Did you fall in love with him?"

"Who me?" Chantilly spoke a little too quickly. "No way." A wave of red spread across her neck, convincing Haley that Chantilly was being less than truthful.

Had Chantilly been responsible for the death of Agnes O'Reilly? She was the first person to happen upon the crime scene. In fact, she might've been the one to hold the pillow over Miss O'Reilly's face and pull the trigger.

If that were the case, what had Chantilly done with the gun? Haley made a mental note to ask Detective Cluney if a weapon had ever been found.

Chantilly squirmed under Haley's scrutiny. "I should go. I don't want to make Madame mad."

Haley agreed, and as they got up, Haley caught sight of another man talking with Mike Tobin at the bar. Of average height and weight, the man wore a flat cap that sat above his ears. The right one which faced Haley was deformed. It was the man she'd encountered on the docks, carrying the suspicious box. He tilted his head to the left as Mr. Tobin spoke.

The man must've come in through the back door. Was he bootlegging for Mike Tobin? Why else would he not enter the tavern from the main entrance like every other customer?

An irate Madame Mercier greeted them at the brothel door. She was dressed in a form-fitting evening gown, hair done to perfection and make-up thickly applied. Clearly she was about to go out—must be a very special client, Haley mused—and was waiting on Chantilly's return.

"Chantilly! You know you have a curfew."

"It's my fault for keeping her out," Haley said.

Chantilly scampered past the madam and scurried up the stairs.

Madame Mercier narrowed her eyes with suspicion. "She was with you the whole time?"

Haley nodded, though it wasn't technically true. She understood how things worked in this house. The girls wouldn't be allowed to have clients on the side. Madame Mercier demanded her cut of the earnings.

"Very well." Madame Mercier started to close the door, but Haley propped her arm against it.

"A quick question, if you don't mind. I noticed a pair of men's shoes in the room where both Snowflake and Primrose died. Do you know who they belong to? Did a client leave them behind?"

"I don't know what you're talking about."

"There was a pair of men's sh—"

"I heard you the first time. Yes. I remember now. Sometimes a client has to leave in a hurry. Perhaps they were forgotten. At any rate they're gone now. I sold them to a man at the market."

Haley had made the mistake of relaxing her stance, and this time she could do nothing when Madame Mercier slammed the door in her face.

16

Samantha stopped briefly at a hotdog stand and ate as she walked from the brothel to the newsroom where she profusely apologized to Mr. August for her long absence.

"Did you at least get a story?" Archie August demanded.

Samantha thought of the photographs she'd shown to Dr. Higgins and realized with chagrin that through all the drama and trauma, she hadn't got an answer to her question: what had the doctor seen in the photographs?

"I got a strong lead," Samantha said.

"A woman dying in childbirth is not a story," Archie August said. He shook his head. "I hope I didn't make a mistake promoting you."

"No, sir, you didn't," Samantha said earnestly. "I promise you, you'll have a story. A great story!"

Archie huffed. "Don't make promises you can't keep, Miss Hawke."

Samantha removed her hat and settled into her desk chair.

Johnny watched her with a smirk. "Hard night, last night, Miss Hawke."

Samantha scowled back. "I'm not late because of that. I was working."

"Oh yeah," Johnny sauntered over to his desk, hands in his pants pockets, shoulders relaxed. Darn that man! She still hadn't forgiven him for interfering with her time dancing with Edoardo. "What are you working on?" Johnny grinned like the mouse who had got the cheese.

"Same thing as you, I presume." Samantha snapped. Then she wondered, maybe Johnny had a new lead. "Did you find out anything more about the Marchesi story?"

"Nah. I was hoping maybe you had."

"If you had butted out last night, maybe I would have."

"Ah, Sam, don't be sore. Besides, I might've done you a favor."

"How so?"

"My pal Tom Bell has taken a shine to you."

Samantha blinked hard, then whispered, "I'm married."

"You're a woman."

"Who is not available."

"So you keep saying, though I don't see no ring on your finger."

"Shh!"

Guiltily, Samantha glanced at her left hand and its bare ring finger. "I take it off for work. I can't very well claim the title 'Miss' while sporting a wedding ring. It's less complicated that way."

Johnny leaned in close. "I have to tell, the guys are starting to talk. Wondering why a pretty girl like you doesn't seem to be interested in men, if you know what I mean."

"Buzz off, Milwaukee! I won't take sass from you or any man. Now leave me alone!"

Johnny Milwaukee never moved an inch. Oh, that man! He could be so infuriating. Samantha opened a file and decided that ignoring her co-worker would be best practice. Not that it ever worked.

"Come on, doll," Johnny said. "I told Bell I'd put in a good word. He's a cop."

Samantha's head shot up. A cop? She hoped to make a contact at the police station.

"Did you tell him I'm m—?" Samantha pinched her lips together, not finishing the M-word.

Johnny shrugged. "He knows your old man skipped town a few years ago."

Samantha couldn't keep the shock off her face. "How does he know that?"

"Don't be so surprised, Sam. It's not like Seth Rosenbaum was a saint. He's got a file six inches thick."

Samantha sighed. It was naïve of her to believe her private life was at all private; that her co-workers were unaware of her husband, or his nefarious past, and that her byline was phony.

"If I agree to go out with him," she began, "what's in it for you?"

Johnny had the nerve to look insulted.

"Nothing. Just the joy of knowing I've made two friends happy."

"Yeah? I thought *you* wanted to date me."

"I did, but you know what they say. It's not a good idea to mix business with pleasure."

He was definitely getting something out of it, Samantha thought. There was only one way to find out what.

"Fine. I'll go out with your friend, so long as he understands it can never be anything serious."

Johnny's smile pulled up crookedly. "I think he'll take whatever he can get."

Samantha didn't dare leave the newsroom until Archie August had driven away. She watched out the second-story window as the bright round headlights of his Buick disappeared around the corner, then she grabbed her things and skedaddled. She wanted to spend time with Talia and appease Bina before heading out again that night.

Bina and Talia were making sweet buns together. They were so involved in their joint task that they didn't hear Samantha enter. The joy on their faces stirred Samantha's heart. She felt grateful to her mother-in-law for caring for Talia so well, but also couldn't help feeling a little resentful. Samantha was meant to take on the role of mothering Talia. She was the one who should be staying at home and baking with her daughter. She was the one who should be taking her to school and picking her up each day.

The anger she felt for Seth squeezed the breath out of her.

Bina must've sensed that someone was watching—her head turned sharply and her eyes narrowed. "You decided to come home, huh?"

Samantha shifted her shoulders back and she resisted the urge to rub the tension that tightened the back of her neck. "I couldn't get away from work. Some days are like that." She removed her hat and gloves, setting them on the table by the door, and hurried over to Talia and kissed her head.

"We're making cinnamon buns," Talia said with her small voice. "My fingers are all sticky."

"So they are. Come to the sink to wash those pinkies."

"The last tray is in the oven," Bina said. "I'll clean it up, and then we can eat. Leftovers from yesterday. Not that Talia's appetite isn't already ruined with the cinnamon rolls. A little girl can't be expected to wait so long for her dinner."

Samantha ignored her mother-in-law's complaint,

and turned each of the X-shaped taps until the hot blended with the cold. Talia stretched on tiptoes, holding her hands under the stream and Samantha scrubbed the dough off with soap.

"So, how was school today?" Samantha asked.

The joy seeped from her daughter's face, and Samantha kicked herself. Still, she needed to know.

"Okay."

Samantha pressed a tea towel around Talia's fingers. "Did you get teased again?"

"Only at recess."

Inwardly, Samantha groaned. Recess was meant to be fun not a time to endure abuse.

"You put out the cutlery," Samantha said to her, "and I'll do the plates and cups." Setting the table was a shared chore, and Talia seemed to rally with the routine.

They ate stew and dumplings and discussed the approaching Yom Kippur Katan, which was a less elaborate version of Yom Kippur.

"You're coming," Bina stated.

"Why would I? I'm not Jewish."

"But you are the mother of a Jewish girl, at least you would be if you converted like you agreed to after you got married."

"Except that Seth left before I could."

The same issue always came up between the Rosenbaum women. The Jewish line passed through the mother and the fact that Samantha hadn't converted put Talia's ethnicity into question. A situation Bina found intolerable.

"So," Bina said. "You made a vow."

"*He* made a vow. Anyway, I don't want to fight with you, Bina. I'll go if Talia wants me to."

Talia's blue eyes grew round as saucers and flashed with her internal struggle. Samantha could see the battle: please her bubba or please her mother?

Samantha softened her gaze. "It's okay, honey. I don't mind going if it means I get to spend time with my best girl."

Talia looked at Bina and Samantha followed her gaze. Bina's eyes were narrow and commanding. There was no way her granddaughter was going to say no to her.

"I want to go," Talia said.

Bina's lips curled slightly as her aged eyes flashed with perceived victory. Samantha let her have the win. Any time with Talia was a bonus, whether it meant going to a park or a *shul*.

Samantha helped Bina clean up the dishes, then put Talia to bed. After reading *The Little Engine That Could*, Samantha tucked Talia in and watched her daughter fall asleep while softly chanting, "I think I can, I think I can."

Samantha quietly changed back into the evening dress she'd worn when she went to the speakeasy with Johnny. Frowning at her image in the mirror, she realized she couldn't go back wearing the same outfit. She chose a different hat and a pair of red T-strap shoes, and this time, added a belt.

HALEY TOOK her turn to cuddle the baby while Molly made dinner. The swaddled baby boy tucked nicely inside her elbow with his small head in the palm of her hand. When he whimpered, she gently swayed him up and down until he fell back to sleep.

"He really is a miracle," Molly said over her shoulder as she slipped a chicken in the oven to broil.

Haley's mind flashed back to the complicated birth and had to agree.

"Indeed, he is."

Master Proust slept in the makeshift crib, a basket Molly had padded with a quilted blanket, and they were able to enjoy their meal in peace. They'd barely finished eating when he started to fuss. Molly hurried to pick him up as Haley cleared the table and started on the dishes.

"Please, leave the dishes," Molly said.

"Well, if you don't mind."

Molly hummed a tune and kissed the child's head. Haley frowned.

"Don't get attached, Molly. He'll be adopted out soon."

Ellen Proust's family had been contacted, but they

refused to claim the baby. They already had too many mouths to feed, and money was scarce.

"I know," Molly said. "I'm sure I'll be glad of it in the middle of the night."

Haley dried her hands and hung the tea towel to dry. "I have a few things I'd like to do tonight. Will you be okay with the baby for a few hours."

"I'm sure I will. I thought you were finished working for the day."

"I am, but there's someone I want to visit. A friend of the baby's mother."

"Yes, well, you should do that I suppose."

Haley gathered her hat and thin summer gloves, but before she slipped them on, she took a moment to pet Mr. Midnight.

"You have the life of luxury, don't you?"

The cat seemed to grin as his green eyes stared up at her.

"I won't be long," Haley called out to Molly and headed for the door.

Haley was thankful that she owned a car. Most Bostonians still had to rely on public transit and their own two feet. Very few women owned their own vehicle. She put the car into gear and rumbled down Grove Street toward the brothel.

It was true that she wanted to talk to Primrose's friends, but not for the compassionate reasons Haley had led Molly to believe. No, she was returning to the brothel because she had finally realized what was out of place in the photographs.

17

Samantha trod lightly to her front door—waking Bina would surely cause a scene—and padded quietly along the dingy hallway and down the four flights of stairs.

From behind closed doors the sounds of the living mingled together: babies crying, couples fighting, a radio blaring. Samantha stepped eagerly into the warmth of the summer evening. A fresh breeze moved through the passage from the entrance, yet didn't erase the stench of greasy meals and cigarette smoke which hung in the air.

Samantha winced at the thought of spending money on taxi fare, but it was too far to walk. At first, she thought she might not have a choice since she couldn't find a taxi to wave down. Wasn't it always like that? When you weren't looking for something, what you didn't need could be seen everywhere, and when you wanted it, it was nowhere to be found.

Finally, a taxi responded to the raising of her arms. Not long afterward she was standing alone in the stair-well of the speakeasy. She took a deep breath and raised her fist to knock. She could do this.

Samantha's heart pounded as she stood at the door of the speakeasy. The cement steps took her down a hollow well where she was concealed from members of the public walking or driving by. Maybe going out at night as a woman alone was a venture in folly, but she'd already knocked, and the eyes on the other side of the peephole stared back at her.

"The real McCoy," she said quietly. When the door didn't open immediately, Samantha feared the password had changed. *Of course, it would,* she thought. *But how had the patrons learned of the change?* She held her breath, thinking frantically of an excuse as to why she didn't know the correct password when the door clicked open.

The bouncer at the door gave her a quick nod. "I remember you," he said. "Go on in." Once again, the energy of the place hit her hard—the abundance of electric lights, the loud music, the boisterous chatter, the laughter of the guests, and of course, the wild dancing—but it didn't surprise her this time. Determined to appear confident, she slapped on a smile and strolled right up to the bar.

Having observed the behavior of the women on her

last visit, Samantha crossed her legs. *I hope no one notices my hose is rayon and not silk.* She twirled the length of beads around her neck, batted heavily mascaraed eyelashes at the bartender, and ordered a Mary Pickford cocktail even though she didn't know exactly what it entailed. She'd overheard another lady order it, and now anticipated the surprise.

The bartender smiled back. "Coming right up."

As she waited, she turned her back to the bar and leaned against it with her bare elbows.

When the band ended one song and started another, tired couples returned to their seats, and those newly energized took the floor. A slender woman, her hair bleached blond and her outfit risqué, carried a round tray filled with drinks above her head. A cloud of smoke from cigarettes consumed by both sexes hovered above the room like early morning fog.

For a moment, everyone stilled—Edoardo Marchesi had entered the club. He wore a crisp white suit that accentuated his broad shoulders and narrow hips. The pant legs hung loosely and landed on polished Italian leather loafers. A brown fedora sat on his head. Two well-built men flanked him, and Samantha swallowed at the sight of the gun-shaped bulges at their waists. She hoped there'd be no trouble tonight.

Edoardo stepped toward the bar, his eyes flickering with recognition when they spotted her. He didn't come to her as she had hoped, but claimed a table at the other end of the bar, his henchmen sitting with him.

Suddenly Samantha doubted her decision to come alone, rather, to come at *all*.

Had the henchmen been with Eduard last night too? Were they always with him? Or is this a special event?

Her stomach twisted at her impetuousness. Bina was right; one day Samantha's headstrong will would get her into trouble.

Her mental debate on whether she should simply walk out or not was interrupted by a movement that came from Edoardo. He held her gaze and she smiled.

If he crossed the floor alone and he asked her to dance, she knew she'd say yes. And after that? Could she remain clearheaded? Professional?

The bartender slid Samantha's cocktail across the counter, a pretty red drink smelling of rum and pineapple juice, and topped with a maraschino cherry. Samantha dug through her clutch and presented three quarters. She could ill afford to spend even a dime on a drink, but she considered this a work expense and would speak to Mr. August about it later if she had a story.

No, not if. When.

Edoardo Marchesi wasn't the only man in the room that Samantha recognized. Tom Bell stared at her from across the dance floor, a look of displeasure on his face.

Samantha had assumed that Officer Bell had been at the club the other night on his own time. Even cops had to blow off steam. And it wasn't like he'd tried to shut the club down.

But maybe he was there for other reasons? Nefarious ones? It wasn't the first time a cop had been corrupted by cash, especially in these hard times.

Her mind spun, and she lost focus on the room for a moment, so when someone tapped her shoulder, she jumped.

"I do apologize. I never meant to startle you."

Edoardo Marchesi stood close to her, his head tilted down. Samantha had the good sense to feel afraid, but she didn't intend to let Mr. Marchesi know that. She threw back her shoulders, lifted her chin, and smiled.

"My mind wandered." She lifted her drink and sipped it as she studied him.

"I don't see your date. Are you here alone?"

"Maybe."

He leaned in closer and whispered in her ear. "It's dangerous for women to go out alone."

Samantha blinked. Was that a threat? Why did Edoardo feel threatened by her?

"Why is that, Mr. Marchesi?," she replied smoothly, hoping he could see how he'd rattled her. "I'm among friends, aren't I?"

Edoardo chuckled. "You're a plucky one; I'll give you that."

"I'll take that as a compliment," Samantha said.

"What have you heard?"

"What do you mean?"

"You're here for a story."

So he knew she was a journalist. Her stomach knotted at the thought that Edoardo Marchesi had been investigating her too. What else had he learned about her?

"Okay," she said. "I'll be honest. I'd like to know more about your brother."

His brow furrowed. "That's it?"

What else was there?

"Yes. Why were you estranged? What could be so bad that a man would be excommunicated from such an influential family?"

Edoardo leaned casually against the bar. "Rivalries happen in all sorts of families."

"Fair enough. What was the cause of yours?"

"Not that it's any of your business, Miss Hawke, but a man doesn't steal from his brother. Not without consequences. Now if you'll excuse me, I believe I've revealed enough about my personal life."

As Edoardo Marchesi strutted away from Samantha's position at the bar in the club, she wondered if she'd just made herself a powerful enemy. Ruing the fact that she'd paid full price and only drunk half, she pushed her cocktail away. Tonight was not a night to lose control of her senses. The electricity in the room was palpable. Despite the loud jazz music, and the oblivious couples dancing on the floor, tension enveloped the place. Why had Edoardo made such a dramatic entrance displaying his henchmen at his side? Across the room, Samantha caught Tom Bell's eye, and he nodded subtly toward the door. Was he signaling for her to leave?

She shook her head.

He dropped his chin, pursed his lips, then nodded toward the back of the room where the restrooms were. Samantha pushed off of her stool and headed in that direction, dodging an attractive woman in a shimmering blue dress who was laughing with her debonair escort.

A graceful woman in a gorgeous glittering evening dress turned, and Samantha was stunned to see Madame Mercier's face. Samantha averted her eyes before their gazes met and hoped the madam hadn't recognized her. *What was she doing here? Drumming up business?*

"Hello, Officer Bell," Samantha said when they finally faced each other. "Fancy meeting you here again."

His eyes flashed with annoyance, which confused Samantha. Hadn't Johnny just said the officer wanted to take her out on a date? Or maybe what she saw was something more serious. Fear?

"You shouldn't be here," he said.

"Why not? You're here."

"That's different."

"Why? Because you're a man?"

He snorted.

"Might I remind you that you're a police officer frequenting an illegal establishment?"

Officer Bell's jaw dropped, and Samantha stared back pompously.

He stepped closer and spoke in her ear.

"I'm on the job. Now get out unless you want more trouble than you're looking for."

Samantha pulled back and shot him a look. Was he serious? Although, she did sense something was up. Now she could taste a big story. This could be her chance to break it. Leaving was out of the question!

Then again, she had Talia to think about. It would be reckless of her to purposely place herself in danger. But really, how dangerous could it get? If she lingered near the back of the room where she could watch and not be in the middle of things, she should be fine.

"I'm staying, but I'll be careful, I promise." She smiled, then sashayed away, feeling the fringe of her dress slapping defiantly against her legs as she made her way to an empty chair along the wall.

She hadn't made it before shots rang out.

Someone shouted, "It's a raid!"

Samantha dropped to the floor and crawled under the table. The rapid beating of her heart made her catch her breath. Preoccupied with making an impression on Officer Bell, she hadn't even seen the police bolting in through the doors, much less who fired first!

She didn't have time to pity her poor fortune. Glass shattered as the chandelier crashed to the floor.

Gunshots popped as the police fired and rounds were returned. Screams.

During a lull, Samantha dared to peek over the edge of the table.

The woman in the blue dress sobbed over her fallen dance partner. Burly police officers stormed the place and started rounding people up. Samantha quickly scanned the room, sifting through the mayhem in search of Edoardo. She couldn't find him, but one of his henchmen lay on the floor bleeding.

Samantha's pulse pounded in her ears as panic took full force. She had to get out. If the police spotted her, they would arrest her. She couldn't go to jail, not even for one night. Not only did she desperately want to get back to Talia, she knew she'd never hear the end of it from Bina! Plus, Mr. August might fire her, and she really needed this job.

She crawled under tables toward the back door, certain there would be cops watching that entrance and the alley behind it, but if chance was on her side, she might be able to create a distraction and get by unseen.

Samantha kept watch on all the chaos as she crawled. At the very least, she had to get a story for her trouble. Searching above the tables and over her shoulder, she nearly ran into a man lying on the floor. She gasped.

"Officer Bell?" She shook his prone body as if that would startle him back to life. "Officer Bell!"

A soft moan emanated from his mouth. He was alive, but blood was erupting from a bullet hole in his side.

Samantha's heart was in her throat. She was desperate to get out of the club, but she couldn't just leave him. He moaned again, louder this time.

"You're going to be fine," Samantha said, not at all sure that he was. She removed Officer Bell's handkerchief from his jacket pocket, opened his vest and placed the folded square over the wound. Samantha didn't have any official medical training, but she did know that a person could bleed to death if the flow of blood wasn't stopped. Beads of sweat covered his ashen face.

"Tell my mother I love her."

"Shut up! You're not going to die."

The club had grown quiet. The only people left were those who were unlucky enough to have got arrested or, even more unlucky, had died.

She frantically waved her hand. "Over here! Officer down! Get an ambulance!"

18

There were two fresh corpses in the morgue. Haley read about the raid that had taken place at a local speakeasy the night before which had brought on their demise.

> A source from the police force says the raid at an illegal establishment on Franklyn Street had been in the works for some time. Boston's chief prohibition agents claim the club, owned and operated by Mob family son Edoardo Marchesi, had been in their sights since the new year but its exact location had been unknown.

Haley frowned. Edoardo Marchesi, again.

> Without warning, the police stormed the place. Shots were fired resulting in the death of one of the

Marchesi family employees as well as an innocent bystander. Officer Tom Bell of the Boston Police Department was seriously injured. The death of the Italian civilian, whose name has not been released, has the members of Little Italy planning protests.

Though this fiasco is, once again, only a case of prohibition agents doing their jobs, many are protesting against prohibition, declaring it a failed experiment. Federally curated statistics easily obtained by the Freedom of Information Act show that not only has crime significantly increased since the implementation of the 18th amendment, but liquor consumption by Americans has never been higher. Opponents claim that taxpayer dollars are wasted, and that enforcement is inefficient. Even with the so-called Rum Line pushed twelve miles from shore, the rum-running business is going strong.

As one bystander stated, "They close down one speakeasy, and two new ones open within the week."

As of this printing, the Marchesi family has been unavailable for comment. Witnesses state that Edoardo Marchesi was seen at the club on the night of the raid, but his current location is unknown to police.

Haley smiled at the byline: *Sam Hawke.*

Without giving it a second thought, she checked for the number in the telephone book, reached for the receiver, and dialed the *Daily Record.*

The call was connected and when the reception picked up, she stated, "I'd like to speak to Sam Hawke."

A young female responded. "Just a moment, and I'll get her for you."

A few minutes later, Samantha answered, "Sam Hawke."

"Hello, Samantha. This is Haley Higgins. I just finished reading your piece in the *Record,* and I wanted to congratulate you."

"Why, thanks!" Haley heard the sound of a hand muffling the end of the line and then Samantha's voice came back at a lower volume. "I'm using the receptionist's phone. I don't want anyone to overhear, especially Freddy Hall. He's bound and determined to steal my thunder."

"Understood. Maybe we could meet up sometime. I want to compare notes."

"I was thinking the same thing, and I'm ready to get out from the suspicious surveillance I'm under here. Johnny's the only one who believed me when I said I was there."

"You were there?"

"Long story. Are you calling from the morgue?"

"Uh-huh."

"Okay. I have some work I need to finish up here, but I should make it there in a couple of hours."

Haley answered, "I'll be waiting."

Samantha hung up abruptly leaving Haley to listen to static.

Haley made a second call, this time to the police department.

"Please connect me with Detective Cluney. Tell him it's Dr. Higgins on the line."

Momentarily, the detective's gruff voice reached her. "Dr. Higgins? What can I do for you?"

"I'm curious, Detective. Did the police ever find the gun that killed Agnes O'Reilly?"

"The brothel gal? Snowfall?"

Haley held in her annoyance. "Snowflake, and yes."

Detective Cluney didn't even bother to cover the mouthpiece as he shouted out to another officer. "No weapon found at the brothel, right?" Then to Haley. "Nope. Sorry, Doc. Anything else I can do to satisfy that curiosity of yours?"

"That will be all for now," Haley said, forcing politeness. She and Detective Cluney had a professional relationship that could be trying at times.

Unfortunately, without the murder weapon and the possibility of finding fingerprints, Haley couldn't prove or disprove Chantilly's guilt or innocence.

Dr. Guthrie shuffled in just as Haley returned the heavy barbell-like receiver. A newspaper was rolled up under his arm, and Haley was certain that meant he'd seen Samantha's article as well.

Without saying hello, Dr. Guthrie answered the question on Haley's mind.

"The police chief said no autopsy for the Marchesi man. Cause of death is already known. Even the city has to tighten its belt because of the economy these days, and the mayor doesn't want to spend money on thugs. His words." He paused at the door to his office. "I fancy a cup of tea. Would you mind, Dr. Higgins?"

Haley forced a smile. These menial tasks were what the interns were for. Thankfully a new one was due to start today.

Having lived in England before, Haley was familiar with the tea-making technique considered of high importance to the British: warm the teapot, add one teaspoon of leaves for each cup plus an extra for the pot, and pour on boiling water.

Carrying the tray with the teapot, milk, and sugar, along with the porcelain teacup and saucer Dr. Guthrie had brought with him from Chesterton, Haley entered the office. He moved papers out of the way so she could set it down.

"Would you like me to pour?" Haley asked.

Dr. Guthrie grunted. "Please."

"So," Haley started, feeling like she should attempt to be companionable. "Are you feeling settled in Boston?"

Dr. Guthrie harrumphed. "If it weren't for my two grandsons, I'd board the next ship heading home."

Haley felt sympathy for her new boss. Homesickness wasn't fun. She remembered her times working on triage in war-torn France where she desperately longed to return to her family in Brookline.

"Tell me about them," she said. "What are their names?"

"Oh," Dr. Guthrie's gray eyes looked up at Haley in surprise. "Well, there's Philip, he's eight, and Albert, who's six."

After ten minutes of discussion about his grand-children, Dr. Guthrie's mood had brightened considerably.

"That's enough of that," he said. He pushed a stack of files to the edge of his desk. "All this paperwork needs to be filed."

Haley also had paperwork to be filed. Plus, there was one body from the raid waiting in the freezer cabinet.

"The new intern should be arriving shortly. Mr. Thomas Martin, I believe is his name. This will be a perfect task to get him started. In the meantime, I'll prepare for the next autopsy. Would you like to assist?"

Dr. Guthrie grunted and shook his head. "Call me if you find anything of interest."

Haley put a clean apron over her cotton pantsuit. Belted at the waist, the wide pant legs flared over low-heeled pumps. Ginger, her fashionista friend, would have been proud of her. Haley could imagine Ginger's vivacious, English-accented voice saying "Bravo,

Haley! Trousers are all the rage, and splendidly convenient!"

Haley smiled at the thought as she vigorously washed her hands with soap and hot water. She then rolled the body of one Mr. Greenfield from the freezer cabinet. It took a bit of upper body strength to shift the corpse onto the operating slab, but Haley had done it so many times it was as easy as pie.

Mr. Greenfield was handsome, even in death, and Haley couldn't help but mourn a little for the man, and for the young life so needlessly cut short.

The entrance wound of the bullet was obvious in the front of the body, just center and left. It was either a skilled shot or a lucky one. Haley lifted the left shoulder and confirmed that there was no exit wound. She slid a thin, rounded piece of wood, like a slender chopstick, into the wound to confirm directionality. Haley wrinkled her nose. Whoever shot this man had done it from a lower position as if the shooter had been sitting on the floor and had shot upwards at a man on his feet.

Not too surprising, considering the melee that had been reported. Someone armed with a gun could very well have fallen.

Using an apparatus that resembled a pair of pointy-nosed pliers, Haley expertly retrieved the bullet and let it drop into a petri dish. It appeared to be a .22.

Haley continued with the normal Y incision procedure and from everything she could see and measure, Mr. Greenfield had been in perfectly good health.

She'd just completed suturing the last stitch of the autopsy when there was a knock at the door. She hurried to the sink and washed her hands.

Dr. Guthrie's head jutted out the door of his office. "Is that him?"

"Is that who?"

"The blasted intern."

"I think it might be a journalist from the *Boston Daily Record.*"

The doctor's eyes darted to the paper on his desk.

Haley answered his unspoken question. "Yes, the same one who wrote about the raid last night. I invited her over."

His white, bushy eyebrows shot up in surprise. "Sam Hawke's a lady?"

"Yes, she is. Her name is Samantha."

Haley removed her apron, hung it on a nearby hook, and opened the door. As expected, Samantha Hawke stood on the other side.

"Hello, Samantha. Come on in."

Samantha's form-fitting dress clung in places, a frequent malady suffered by women throughout the city due to the humidity, and Samantha pulled at the fabric. "Oh, it's so nice and cool in here. Such a relief." She removed her hat and summer gloves, and placed them on the rack. "The mugginess is driving me crazy.

Born and raised in Boston, you'd think I'd be used to it by now."

"Adaptation is not a given," Haley said. "When air has a high moisture content it hinders the normal perspire and cooling cycle. The human body has to work even harder to cool, resulting in excessive sweating which can result in loss of water and chemicals our bodies need to function properly."

Samantha stared openly and Haley realized belatedly, that she'd fallen into her bad habit of expositing where it wasn't necessary. She added quickly, "Would you like a glass of water?"

Samantha nodded. "Yes, please."

Haley used the sink by the coffee and tea station and filled a glass. She offered it to her guest who took it gratefully.

After a long drink, Samantha's eyes landed on the body still lying on the surgical table in the middle of the room. The sheet was pulled up to the chin, leaving the face exposed.

"Oh, sorry," Haley said. "I'm expecting an intern to arrive any minute and was going to let him put the corpse away." Haley stepped swiftly to the body and pulled the sheet over his head.

"I recognize him," Samantha said soberly. "From the club last night. He'd been dancing with a pretty lady in a lovely blue dress. They were laughing and flirting, and I imagine he thought he had all the time in the world to fall in love. Moments later he was struck down. It's just so sad. So unfair."

"It's always hard when they're young," Haley said. "The question is, who shot him? The police or one of Marchesi's men?"

"Either way, he's still dead."

Haley decided to move the body herself and lifted it onto a trolley. "Who knows when the intern will actually arrive?" She deposited it into one of the freezer compartments and hoped her actions portrayed a desire for efficiency, but she suspected Samantha had caught on that Haley had moved the cadaver out of sight for her benefit.

Once again, Haley thoroughly washed her hands before continuing on to the table where the photographs Samantha had taken were spread out.

Samantha snapped to attention and followed her. "Do tell me you found what you were looking for?"

Haley simply pointed to the crack in the wardrobe door and handed Samantha the magnifying glass.

"A man's shoe?" she asked with a note of skepticism. "That's it?"

"It may not seem like much, but ask yourself—why is there a man's shoe in the wardrobe of the boudoir? Wouldn't a man leave with the shoes on his feet that he came with?"

Samantha held the magnifying glass over the image again for a second look. "I suppose so. Still, it doesn't seem like much of a clue."

Haley chortled. "The smallest clues are the ones that usually break a case."

Samantha's eyes darkened with a look of interest and curiosity. "You sound like you've had a lot of experience solving murder cases."

"I've helped to solve a few." Haley wasn't being humble. How could she boast about her amateur detective skills when her own brother's case lay cold as the Atlantic in January. She changed the subject. "Congratulations again on your story in the *Record*."

"Thanks," Samantha gushed. "I won't lie. It felt great to get the boss's attention and commendation, especially in front of an office full of egotistical men."

Haley held in a smile. She motioned to an empty chair. "Please have a seat and tell me all about what happened at the club."

19

———

Samantha was intrigued by her new friend. Perhaps "friend" was too strong a word. Acquaintance. Dr. Haley Higgins held Samantha at arm's length, and the wall between them, though thin, was present. Samantha wondered if the doctor was like this with everyone, or was there something about her specifically that she didn't like.

"You went alone?" Haley asked, stopping Samantha before she'd barely even got started relating the events from the night before.

"Yes. I'd been there before, with Johnny—Mr. Milwaukee—so I knew what I was getting into. Many women go to clubs without dates, usually with other women, granted, but it wasn't like my gender was greatly outnumbered. In fact," Samantha found herself leaning in even as Haley leaned back, "they drink, smoke, and dance as freely as the men."

Samantha hoped to have shocked the upright doctor, but Haley didn't even blink. Of course, there was probably no sin or vice that Dr. Higgins hadn't encountered in her line of work. It was Samantha who had been surprised at first, but now she felt a little worldly. She couldn't help but think that Haley Higgins could use a night out to loosen up.

"I was sitting at the bar when Edoardo Marchesi approached me."

Besides the lifting of a dark brow, Haley didn't interrupt. Samantha relayed everything that had followed, his strange, confronting conversation, the disgruntled stares of Officer Tom Bell from across the room, the raid, how she'd hid. Finding Tom Bell injured on the floor.

"I'm glad to hear that Officer Bell is going to recover," Haley said. "I've learned something interesting about the Marchesis as well."

Samantha's reporter instincts clicked in, and she pushed a strand of blond hair behind her ear and listened.

"Stefano Marchesi was the father of Agnes O'Reilly's baby."

"Snowflake? No!" Samantha couldn't contain her shock. "Really? How do you know this?"

"I had a conversation with the second victim's friend, Chantilly. It seems Stephen March was quite the ladies' man, and not too careful about it, I might add. Chantilly insists that Miss O'Reilly and Mr. March were in love."

"But still, how can they be sure?"

"It doesn't matter if Stefano was *actually* the father," Haley replied, "only that they *believe* that he is."

"Ah, I see," Samantha said. Perception was everything. "Maybe Primrose killed Snowflake. It's certainly motive since Primrose's encounter with March was obviously before Snowflake's."

"That thought crossed my mind too," Haley said. "Are you postulating that Primrose killed Mr. March as well?"

Samantha lifted her shoulder. "You know what they say about a woman scorned."

"Yet, the witness said a man entered the tavern moments before Mr. March was shot down," Haley added.

"Ah. The shoes!" Of course, Samantha thought. "Primrose dressed up as a man. Did the witness say if the man was fat?"

"I don't think so, but that doesn't mean anything," Haley said. "Some witnesses don't give out details unless specifically asked. It's quite possible that Primrose, or maybe another woman, did indeed pose as a man, entered the Bell in Hand, and shot Mr. March. Unfortunately, Madame Mercier has already disposed of the evidence."

Samantha narrowed her eyes grimly. "Son of a

gun!"

Haley's gaze flittered upward in thought.

"What?" Samantha asked.

"When I was at the Bell in Hand with Chantilly, I saw a man speaking to Mr. Tobin."

"The waiter?"

"Yes," Haley confirmed. "Mr. Tobin, the waiter at the tavern. I didn't see the man come in through the front door, which makes me presume he came in from the employees' entrance. Mr. March was a rum runner, and I'm quite sure this fellow is too. As much as Mr. Tobin protests, I'm fairly certain he's being supplied with contraband. Keeping our net wide, I think it might be a good idea to talk to him."

"What did he look like?" Samantha asked.

"Average height and weight, unkempt. His right ear was deformed, and the way he turned his left ear to Mr. Tobin when he spoke makes me believe he's hard of hearing in the right. I'd actually met him before when I went to the wharf."

"I've met him too!" Samantha said. "When Mr. Milwaukee and I went to Long Wharf to ask a few questions, a man that fits that description was working with Bobby Ryan. It was hard to miss that ear."

"Bobby Ryan, the unnamed man with the bad ear, and Mike Tobin. They're all connected somehow."

"Mr. Ryan and his buddy bring in the contraband and Mr. Tobin sells it," Samantha said.

"I'm fairly certain Mr. Tobin has been a client at

the brothel," Haley said.

"Mr. Ryan as well." Samantha relayed how she'd seen Bobby Ryan and Madame Mercier together at the market.

Samantha watched as Haley took in this information. Something flickered behind her brown eyes, and she wrinkled her brow as if in deep thought.

"What is it?" Samantha asked.

Haley's focus cleared. "I think I know who the killer is."

Samantha shouted, "Who?"

Haley hesitated and Samantha could see apprehension in her eyes. The doctor was reluctant to speak a name without proof. Before Samantha could convince her to confide in her, they were interrupted by a knock on the door. It slowly opened, and the figure of a slim male in his twenties stepped in. He removed his hat then said, "Hello, I'm Thomas Martin."

"Yes," Haley said, standing. "We've been expecting you. I'm Dr. Higgins, assistant medical examiner, and this is my associate, Miss Hawke."

So, that's the word, Samantha thought. They were *associates*. Now she just wished her associate would tell her who she thought had killed Stefano Marchesi. Darned poor timing on Mr. Martin's part!

Haley answered the intern. "Dr. Guthrie is in his office. Go on in, and introduce yourself."

Samantha followed Haley's gaze through the glass wall of Dr. Guthrie's office where the three of them stared at the strange, long-limbed man who housed a mass of wild gray hair. His long chin rested on his chest, and his eyes fluttered closed.

"Oh, yes, all right," Mr. Martin muttered cautiously. Then he pivoted to face Haley. "I almost forgot. I'm sorry, just with meeting you and I confess to being a little nervous."

"What did you forget?" Haley asked kindly.

"Your taxi is here. The driver asked me to tell you."

Haley looked at Samantha with confusion. "That's odd," she said.

Samantha didn't understand. "What's odd?"

"I didn't order a taxi."

"ARE YOU READY?" Haley said. Proverbial butterflies fluttered in her chest as they often did when she felt she was close to closing a case. "We can take my car."

"Take your car where?" Samantha asked.

"To the brothel. We need a bit more information."

Samantha collected her messenger bag and camera bag. "Can I borrow your phone to let Mr. August know what I'm up to?Otherwise, he's bound to sack me."

"You can use the one on my desk." Haley hated to waste the taxi driver's time and wanted to clear up the misunderstanding. "I'll meet you outside."

Haley walked quickly down the whitewashed hallways of the hospital and up the steps. She felt bad about leaving Mr. Martin alone with Dr. Guthrie on his first day. Dr. Guthrie's personality was best explained.

She'd reached the main floor when a male voice called out to her. "Dr. Higgins."

Haley stopped and turned. The voice belonged to geriatrician Dr. Gerald Mitchell. He was taller than Haley, had salt-and-pepper hair oiled back, and possessed a pleasant face. He had good manners and loved going to places like the opera, live theater, and more recently talking pictures. Haley knew this because she often accompanied him to such events.

She smiled as he approached.

"It's been busy in the basement," he said with a chuckle. Gerald had warm brown eyes that twinkled and an excellent bedside manner. His patients loved him.

"Yes. Some weeks are like that."

"How's the new ME?" He inclined his head and lowered his voice and teased, "Should I be worried?"

Haley and Gerald had an easy friendship. He had recently celebrated eighteen years of marriage to Elsa who'd suffered a serious stroke in 1926 and remained in a vegetative state. They had no children.

Gerald was devoted to his wife, so his companionship with Haley had remained platonic. He liked to go out on the town, but not alone, he'd said. Even for someone as naturally cheerful as Dr. Mitchell, he found attending cultural events alone depressing.

Haley didn't mind the arrangement. She wasn't the marrying kind, or rather, she was married to her work. She also found it dreary to go out on her own, and she enjoyed Gerald Mitchell's company.

"I should hardly think so," she replied. "Dr. Guthrie is too old, even for me. I knew him in England, you know?"

"How coincidental!"

"Isn't it?"

"Anyway, I'm speaking at a fundraiser for the geriatrics department tonight," Gerald said. "I didn't mention it before because I thought you might find it boring. Then when I saw you just now, I realized *I* might find it boring. Would you consider rescuing me from such a fate? I realize it's rather last minute, but the food promises to be stupendous. If you're busy with something else, I understand."

"I'd be happy to come to your aid, Dr. Mitchell," Haley said. She could use a short diversion from her work.

"Terrific. I'll pick you up at seven."

"I'll be ready."

Samantha caught up with her just as Dr. Mitchell had bid her farewell. She looked at Haley in confusion.

"I thought you were releasing the cabbie?"

"Oh, yes!" With Gerald Mitchell capturing her attention, Haley had completely forgotten. "He's probably already picked up another fare."

They hurried outside, and the glare of the midday

sun momentarily blinded them. Before Haley could speak to the cabbie, who'd been waiting patiently—straw hat tilted over his face as if he were trying to catch a quick wink before his next fare—Samantha touched her arm. Haley turned around.

"We didn't talk about what to do next," Samantha said. "As a reporter, I should probably know, but this is my first case, and you've had many. Help a gal out. What should I do next?"

Haley empathized with Samantha's nerves. The drive to do a good job—no, a perfect job—could be debilitating. "Let me talk to the cab driver first."

Haley stepped to the window, reached in, and poked the man's shoulder. Lightning fast, he grabbed her arm, causing Haley to yelp in surprise. Then she saw the gun—a beautiful Harrington & Richardson .22 nine-shot pistol with a six-inch barrel and walnut checkered grip. Haley recognized the gun because she had one just like it locked in her desk drawer at the morgue.

The man raised his head, and Haley suffered another shock when she stared into the eyes of Madame Mercier.

Haley muttered, "I knew it."

Gone was the madam's French accent. "Whatcha do next is git in the taxi."

Haley's instinct was to tell Samantha to run, but Madame Mercier's next words stopped her.

"I know Miss Hawke has a daughter, and I know

where she lives."

A quick look back at Samantha confirmed that she had overheard. Before Haley could do anything to stop her, Samantha was in the backseat.

Madame Mercier waved the H&R pistol at Haley. "Git in and drive. Don't think of doing anything crazy or I'll shoot your friend."

Haley glanced about her hoping to see someone she knew, desperate to give some signal that they were in danger, but there was no one and nothing she could do. Cars zoomed by and pedestrians walked about like there was nothing at all out of the ordinary, like there wasn't a madwoman in the taxi waving a gun.

Madame Mercier slid over to the passenger seat. She had her pistol pointed at Samantha and any thoughts Haley had about refusing flew out the window. Why had Samantha rushed to obey? They could've gotten a hand up on their captor if she'd only run away instead of jumping into the backseat. There was only one possibility: Madame Mercier had hit the mark and Miss Hawke was indeed a mother.

Haley got in and closed the door. She placed a hand on the steering wheel and the other on the gearshift. She stared hard at Madame Mercier. The woman's eyes were hard and cruel.

"Where are we going?" Haley asked. Her voice sounded sure and unwavering, but inside she was trembling.

20

Samantha felt as if someone was sitting on her chest. This awful, evil woman had threatened Talia! Samantha had never been one for guns, and she most definitely had never had one pointed at her point-blank. Her peripheral vision blurred, and she was frantic not to let herself faint.

"What do you want? Just tell us what you want, and we'll give it to you!"

Gripped with shallow rapid breaths, in and out, she panted like a dog. Samantha couldn't get her breath. She was going to black out. She'd die before Madame Mercier could even pull the trigger!

"Samantha!" Haley's voice pulled her back to her senses. "Breathe into your hands. You're hyperventilating."

Samantha cupped her palms and held them over her mouth. After a few terrifying seconds, her breath started to ease, and along with it her extreme panic. Haley Higgins was with her. She was calm and collected. She'd know what to do to get out of this mess.

Talking would help her get a hold of her nerves. "You killed Stefano Marchesi! Dressed like a man, like you are now, you walked into the Bell in Hand and killed him."

Madame Mercier's eyes narrowed and flashed with hatred. "He betrayed me. He was supposed to love me! He—" She cut herself off and shook her head.

Samantha caught Haley glancing back at her in the rearview mirror. With a slight nod, she encouraged her to keep talking.

Samantha roused up every bit of bravery she could muster. "What about Snowflake? Did she betray you too?"

Madame Mercier laughed. "You know she did. That spawn was Stephen's."

"And Primrose? She carried Mr. March's baby too. Why didn't you shoot her as well?"

"Because of the size of the child! I'm not a monster. And providence took care of her for me anyway."

Madame Mercier had directed Haley to take them back to her townhouse on Endicott Street. When the place drew close, she waved the nose of the pistol and said, "The back alley."

The lane that ran behind the row of houses was only wide enough for one vehicle at a time. Two ruts were worn in the dirt, and Haley struggled with the large steering wheel to keep the car aligned. Tired wooden fences flanked the alley and leaned precariously from years of wind and the heavy weight of wet winter snow. Wild grass reached skyward between the planks of wood, with summer wildflowers blooming in all the colors of the rainbow.

One lone lopsided gate was propped open, a forethought by their captor.

"Turn here," Madame Mercier demanded. "And park."

There wasn't much of a backyard, and what was there had been uncared for. Only the front yard and the interior were necessary for appearance's sake, Samantha supposed.

Madame Mercier threatened them once again. "Now put your hands on your heads and git out. And no funny stuff. I've got plenty of bullets to go around."

Samantha shuffled out of one side and Haley out of the other. Samantha wondered if Madame Mercier meant to lock them up in her house, but it was worse than that. She spied a cellar door opened up against the back wall.

Madame Mercier caught her looking. "That's right. Go on down, the both of yous." Samantha walked around the nose of the taxi, noting the bug splatters that covered the large round headlights and the dirty grille. If only there were some way she and Haley could disarm Madame Mercier. As it was, the madam had been clever enough to keep her distance, and she never dropped her guard when it came to her gun.

The cellar was musty and cool. At least the change in temperature provided a physical comfort. Samantha felt soaked from the natural humidity in the air combined with nervous sweat. The only light came from the rays of sun that cut through the immediate darkness.

Madame Mercier backed up the steps, her pistol at the ready. "Make yourselves comfortable," she said before closing the cellar door above and throwing them into darkness.

THERE WAS a small crack of light coming from the cellar door that illuminated the steps, but behind them, everything was black. Haley became aware of Samantha's breath, once again growing shallow and rapid. She said softly, "Breathe into your hands."

Samantha's breath became muffled, and Haley knew she was doing as instructed. Haley kept her eyes on the crack of light and pushed on the doors, but beyond a slight buckle, it wouldn't move. Madame Mercier had padlocked them in.

Maybe there was another way out. Some cellars could be accessed from inside the house as well as outside.

"Samantha, you should sit on the steps."

"Are you going to sit on the steps?"

"No. I'm going to search the cellar for another way out."

"It's pitch black."

"I know."

"What about mice and spiders? This place is full of cobwebs."

"I'll take the risk."

"Then I will too."

Haley was glad it was dark at that moment. She wouldn't have wanted Samantha to see the doubt that tightened across her face.

"Very well. You start on the right side of the steps, and I'll start on the left. We're looking for some change in the wall feature, the outline of a door or panel—a doorknob or latch.

The rough concrete of the cold room snagged the tips of her fingers, and Samantha had been right—there were plenty of cobwebs. Every couple of seconds Haley had to rub her face along her arm to clear it of sticky silk and loose dust that showered down.

On the other side of the cellar, Haley heard soft moans of disgust and outright fear. "Find anything?" Haley asked.

"No. Just a row of empty shelves with who knows what growing on it."

She admired Samantha's determination to push through her obvious phobia. The tremor in her voice had receded. Haley thought it would be good to keep her talking.

"I didn't know you had a daughter."

A pause, and then, "It's not something I advertise. I've gone to work as a single woman not a single mother. No one will hire a married woman, so I went back to my maiden name."

"Is your husband deceased?"

A harsh chortle. "No. He robbed a pharmacy and skipped town."

"Oh, I didn't know."

"Yeah, well, it's another thing I don't like to boast about. Haven't laid eyes on him for six years, so for all I know, he could be dead."

"Tell me about your daughter?"

"Her name is Talia. She's six. Beautiful. Smart as a whip."

By now they had both made it to the back wall and were closing in. So far, no second exit.

Then Samantha screamed.

A cold shiver raced down Haley's spine. She called into the darkness. "What is it? Are you okay?"

"I think a mouse just ran up the back of my leg!"

Haley let out a short breath of relief. "Shake it off."

"What do you think I'm doing? A flippin' swing dance in the dark, is what!"

"Is it gone?"

"Yes, I think so."

"Who takes care of her when you're working?"

"What?"

Haley wanted to keep Samantha distracted. "Your daughter. Who watches her when you're not home?"

"My mother-in-law. Bina Rosenbaum drives me crazy, but she's good with Talia. Bina loves her as much as I do. I owe my mother-in-law a lot, but she's just so— stubborn, and belittling. She never thought I was good enough for her son, because I'm not Jewish."

Haley suddenly saw Samantha in a new light. "I owe you an apology."

"Why?" Samantha said.

"I've misjudged you terribly. I assumed you were just another ruthless journalist who didn't care who they stepped on to get a story—that you were one of those modern women with something to prove. I thought you were weak. But you're a working single mother, the toughest and strongest type of woman there is."

There was a beat before Samantha answered. "Thank you. I've misjudged you too."

Haley braced herself. It wasn't easy to hear about other people's negative perceptions about who you were. Yet, if you were about to die, it was a good time to clean the slate.

Samantha's words reached her through the blackness. "I thought you were clinical and unfeeling. Angry about something or hurt, and burying yourself in your work so you wouldn't have to face it."

"You didn't misjudge me," Haley said. "Your

reporter instincts have hit the bull's-eye." If Haley was going to clear her slate, she'd better do it.

"My brother Joseph was murdered back in '24. I have three brothers, but he and I were the closest in age, and we were pals growing up. I was a tomboy, and to him, I was just another brother—at least until I hit a certain age. We played baseball, shot squirrels, fished in the river, worked on the farm. It was like we were twins, sharing the same soul.

"I was living in London when it happened, but came back to Boston immediately. I worked with the police, hired my own private investigator, did my own sleuthing, everything I could to find out who murdered my brother and bring him to justice."

"You never found who killed him?" Samantha said. They were standing side by side now.

"No," Haley answered. "The case is cold and forgotten."

Haley took Samantha by the elbow, and together they shuffled toward the line of light seeping through the cellar door, and collapsed on the steps where they did the only thing left they could do. Wait.

Time passed, but the light in the crack remained strong. With the long summer days it was hard to know what time it was, yet with the rumbling of her stomach, Haley guessed they were into the evening. Haley's only hope now was that Gerald would grow concerned when he came to pick her up at seven and, on not finding her, would call for a search. Maybe Samantha's boss would worry too. And Samantha's uptight mother-in-law might sound an alarm as well.

The fact that Madame Mercier hadn't brought them anything to eat or drink didn't bode well. It meant she didn't intend to keep them alive. Haley hoped she didn't mean to leave them in the cellar to die of thirst. Haley knew enough about how the body mechanics worked when deprived of water to feel truly distressed. Her parched throat was made worse from the fine dust they'd stirred up in their search for a way out. Tired of doing nothing, Haley had even made a grid of the small room, shuffling like a blind woman, arms stretched out, hoping to come across something that could be used as a weapon, but the cellar had been completely cleared out. The advent of electric refrigeration in the convenience of your own kitchen made outdoor treks to cold-storage cellars less necessary.

The line of light eventually faded to darkness. Though Haley couldn't see Samantha, she knew her companion lay on her back across one of the steps, having given in to her fatigue some time ago.

"I'd die for a glass of water," Samantha finally said, then chuckled thickly. "Bad choice of words."

Haley commiserated. "I feel like I swallowed a sock."

"Speaking of socks, my poor stockings are ruined." Haley heard Samantha sit up, and rustle about. "I might as well just take them off."

Haley was glad she'd worn her pantsuit.

The removal of Samantha's stockings was quick. "There you go, mice. Make a nest."

They heard voices overhead and the rattle of a key turned in the lock. The cellar door slammed open, and a bright light kept them blinded. Haley cupped her eyes and eventually made out the male figure peering down, aiming Madame Mercier's revolver at them. It was Bobby Ryan from the Long Wharf.

He held up two sets of handcuffs, then tossed them down. "Put these on."

21

A swath of dark clouds shielded the moon, and the cooling breeze stirred the leaves in the trees. Rain fell in softly, and Samantha tilted her head back, mouth open wide, eager to lap up every little drop.

A torturous bright light streamed into her eyes, and she squinted back at the source. Madame Mercier's impatient voice revealed the owner of the flashlight. "Come on, git in the car!"

Samantha felt helpless. She and Haley were handcuffed and held at gunpoint. They were going to be taken somewhere and killed. Samantha held back a sniffle. She should've spent more time saying goodbye to Talia that morning. How was she to know it was the last time she'd ever see her daughter?

Madame Mercier handled the pistol while Bobby Ryan drove. With their hands cuffed behind their

backs, neither Samantha nor Haley could brace themselves as Bobby steered recklessly around corners,
forcing them to lean into each other. The electric lamp-
posts made it clear where they were headed—back to
Long Wharf.

"Where'd you get a taxi from?" Haley said.

Samantha was glad Haley had asked. It wasn't like
you could just rent a taxi to use whenever you
wanted one.

Madame Mercier reverted to her French accent.
"Zere are fellas who'll do anysing for me."

This fake French woman was getting on Samantha's last nerve. "Like shooting the outside of the
building to conceal that you shot a man in cold blood
from inside?"

Madame Mercier settled a steely gaze on Samantha. Then she stroked the side of Bobby Ryan's face.
"Like I said, I got fellas."

Samantha had never understood how men could
be so obsessed with a woman that they'd risk going to
prison or taking the death penalty. Seth Rosenbaum
certainly wouldn't have done that for her, the bum.

In the daytime, Long Wharf was busy and noisy
with people coming and going, shouting instructions,
and starting up truck engines. Ships glided in and out
blasting their horns to announce their intentions.

At night, the wharf was as quiet as a cemetery with
only the lapping of the waves hitting the dock resound-
ing. An odd light shone through the row of brick ware-

houses situated along the length of the wharf where someone was working late. Even if they happened to look out the window, they wouldn't see Madame Mercier's car because Bobby Ryan had parked behind a loading bin.

There was a boat moored near the shore, a schooner with chipped and weatherworn white and sky-blue paint. The word *Maelstrom* was scrawled along the side in hand-painted script. Standing on the deck was the fellow with the cauliflower ear.

Bobby Ryan parked the car, got out, and opened the back door on Samantha's side.

Madame Mercier barked, "Git out."

This was bad.

Samantha's heart raced like rats in a gutter, and she could barely swallow. She shimmied out of the car—Haley doing the same right behind her—and made an effort to stand. Her knees quivered, and she hoped she wasn't about to faint. The salty air stung her eyes, and she couldn't help the tears that leaked out. With all the mascara she'd put on that morning, she didn't doubt that she looked like a wet raccoon

"Hey, Boyle," Madame Mercier said as they drew closer to the vessel. "I have a package for you to deliver."

Boyle, the man with the bad ear, looked on Samantha and Haley with black eyes. Chapped lips curled cruelly. "Certainly."

Bobby Ryan removed a small key from his pants

pockets and taunted them with it. "No use in losin' two perfectly good sets of cuffs." He removed Samantha's first, then Haley's and they both furiously rubbed circulation back into their wrists.

Madame Mercier had her revolver trained on them. "Git in, both of you."

Samantha knew that if they got on the boat, their chances of surviving would drastically decrease, but Madame Mercier was unhinged, and the slightest provocation could cause an impulsive pulling of the trigger.

Haley nodded at Samantha to go ahead. Samantha admired the doctor's nerve. Thinking about Talia and how she had to survive this for her daughter, Samantha gathered her courage.

She walked the plank onto the boat.

Boyle's shirt was unbuttoned revealing a stained undershirt. His face was leathery due to many years working outdoors on the ocean, and bristles darkened his jaw. He had a deformed ear, but that wasn't the most notable thing about him. It was the handle of a gun that stuck out of the waistband of his pants. He was quick to bind Samantha's wrists with rope, knotting her securely to the metal rail. At least this time her hands were bound in front and not behind her back. He repeated his performance on Haley, tying her to the other side of the boat.

Bobby Ryan shouted to Boyle. "You know what to do."

Boyle responded with a mock salute. "Twelve miles out."

Twelve miles out was the rum-running line where prohibition agents no longer had jurisdiction or authority to arrest. Samantha wondered if Boyle was scheduled to make a liquor pick up, and was simply doing double duty by tossing a couple of bodies overboard while he was at it.

Madame Mercier had already disappeared, but Bobby Ryan paused before taking his leave to stare at the two captives. "Such a shame, two beautiful specimens such as yous guys." He tutted, then left them alone with Boyle who mocked them by drinking heartily from a pop bottle.

STANDING on a slippery boat while it slammed along the waves would be impossible so Haley guided herself down the side of the fishing boat until she was seated on the wet floor. She winced as the cold dampness seeped through her pantsuit. Goosebumps sprouted on her arms, which were now elevated above her head.

Samantha mimicked the maneuver.

From this position Haley could see Boyle through the opened cabin door, propped on one knee, and with one hand on the wheel. His position was angled in such a way that he could keep an eye on where he was going and on the two captives. His gun was evident on the seat beside him.

Haley started taking inventory. Tucked in the cubbyhole behind her was a rag, a flare gun kit, and discarded trash. Near the back, closer to where Samantha was positioned sat a large tackle box. Haley would bet a hundred dollars that beneath it was a hidden door that opened to cargo space where they stored the illegal liquor. A pair of oar handles jutted out of the cubbyhole behind Samantha. One donut-shaped life preserver was secured to the wall.

Haley gave Samantha a meaningful look and nodded toward the tackle box. Surely, there must be a tool inside that could help them—a fishing knife, perhaps.

Samantha started shifting her body toward the back, easing the knot that tied her hands above her head, now slippery in the drizzling rain, along the rail. She got as far as the next bolt which prevented her from getting closer. Her eyes beseeched Haley, and Haley pointed her toes in response. Samantha got the message and stretched out her legs. With the tip of her shoe, Samantha was just able to reach it.

Haley wished that she could switch places with her. For once, Haley's long legs could've come in handy.

Samantha groaned with the effort, and Haley was glad the sound of the engine drowned her out. Haley's gaze kept flitting toward the cabin and her view of

Boyle as if she could will him to stay put and focused on the waves in front of him with the power of her mind.

Samantha mouthed, "I did it!"

Haley's attention became riveted to the toolbox and Samantha's shoe threaded through the handle.

Haley held her breath. If Samantha could ease the tool kit close enough, she might be able to flip open the lid and somehow fish a knife out with her toes.

The wooden box proved to be heavier than it looked, and Samantha tugged on the handle with considerable effort. It made a screeching sound across the surface of the boat's floor, and for a second she froze.

Pulling the box toward her, Samantha discarded the shoe and worked on opening the latch with her toes. Handy that she no longer had to contend with stockings, Haley thought. Samantha propped open the lid. "I see a knife!"

Haley's gaze darted back at the cabin. Boyle was looking ahead, but just as Haley motioned for Samantha to continue, he turned.

"Hey!"

Samantha jerked her foot, and the lid snapped shut. She shot Haley a panicked look.

Suddenly, the sound of the engine went quiet. With both feet Samantha pushed the tackle box back a split second before Boyle stormed out of the cabin. With the motor off, the silence that encircled them was the call of death. He pointed his weapon back and forth between the women. Samantha was splayed along the floor, her dress twisted around her torso, and her eyes glued on their captor. His rubber boots gripped the surface as he marched toward her. Samantha curled into a ball as he pointed his gun at her head.

"What are you silly women doing? I'll kill you, you understand."

"Wait," Haley shouted. She needed to divert Boyle's attention before he figured out what they were up to. "She was throwing up over the edge and slipped. That's all."

"Huh?" Boyle turned his head so his good ear faced her.

Haley repeated loudly, "She was throwing up over the edge and slipped."

Boyle pivoted and in a flash pressed the gun muzzle under Haley's chin. "The only reason I don't kill the both of yous right now is cuz I don't want to get my boat dirty. But I wouldn't tempt me if I was yous."

"You have our word," Haley muttered.

"What?"

She shouted this time. "You have our word!"

Boyle went back to his position at the front of the boat and started the engine.

Samantha pulled herself back into a seated position. Sounding defeated she said, "We're going to hit the twelve-mile mark any minute, and he's going to throw us overboard."

"I know." Impulsively, Haley looked to Boyle who'd started up the engine again, and when his gaze was focused out to sea, she said to Samantha, "I have an idea."

22

_H_aley shouted her plan over the engine noise, careful not to talk too loudly and attract Boyle's attention. But first, Samantha had to get that fishing knife.

For a second time, Samantha stretched out her body along the floor of the boat. She grimaced, and Haley knew the strain on her up-stretched arms would be painful. Samantha pointed the bare toes of her right foot and snagged the handle of the tackle box. Carefully, she shifted it along the damp surface until it was close enough to open.

Haley held her breath as Samantha, with both feet working together, managed to lift the knife out of the box and drop it to the floor. Swiftly she closed the lid again and pushed the box back into position.

The engine stuttered and with her foot, Samantha

impulsively shot the knife over to Haley, who then shifted her body to conceal it.

Boyle stood at the doorway of the cabin, eyeing them suspiciously. Both Haley and Samantha were in position, hands tied to the railing over their heads. Boyle huffed before returning to his seat.

That was close, Haley thought.

Now for her own circus act. She rose to her knees and worked to get the handle of the knife pinned between them. Returning to a seated position, she lifted the knife with her knees and carefully grabbed the handle with her mouth. She forced herself to not gag on the stench or at the thought of the invisible germ colony that lived there.

Next Haley returned to her knees and painstakingly sawed at the rope that pinned her wrists together. She hoped and prayed Boyle wouldn't grow suspicious, and if he spotted her like that, he'd assume she was taking a turn at vomiting over the edge.

It felt like an eternity, but within minutes the rope around her wrists unraveled. She looked over her shoulder at Samantha and grinned.

Haley took a quick moment to rub some feeling back into her arms. Keeping her back angled toward Boyle, she reached for the flare gun kit and opened it to find a flare gun and two flares inside. She removed the gun and loaded it. Her blouse had pulled loose from the waist of her pants, and if she kept her back turned toward the cabin, she could manage to conceal the gun

LEE STRAUSS

from Boyle. Now they had to wait until they reached the twelve-mile line and he came after them. She put her arms back up over her head and hung onto the rail.

The engine cut.

"This is it!" Boyle proclaimed. "The end of the line for you ladies."

This was the moment of truth—would their plan work? Haley wondered. She faced Boyle and without making a sound, mouthed, "What?"

Boyle, looking confused, swung his gun from Haley to Samantha. In turn, Samantha silently mouthed, "Don't hurt us!"

Boyle slapped his head as if he was knocking the wax out of his ear. In that instant, his hand holding the pistol grew slack, and went off target. It was a split second, but long enough. Haley produced the flare gun and fired. The force of the flare knocked Boyle's gun out of his hand and it slid to the back of the boat, lodging behind the tackle box. Boyle jumped and yelled in pain at what would be a nasty burn. He spun out of control as he held his arm, knocked against the rail next to where Haley sat and at that precise moment, the boat bobbed through a large wave. Boyle lost his balance and promptly fell overboard.

Boyle's cries reached them. "Help!"

The life preserver was next to Samantha. Haley hurried to the other side of the boat. If she didn't toss it overboard, Boyle would drown.

Death at the Tavern

Samantha, still tied to the rail, stared at Haley with a stern expression. "Do you have to?"

"We're not murderers," Haley said. "So, yes."

With the skill of a champion softball player, Haley threw the life preserver to Boyle. The boat had drifted away from him and at first, it looked like he wasn't going to reach it. Whether the man lived or died now depended on how well he could swim. Then as if by a divine hand, a wave pushed the preserver right in front of him.

"Great, he's saved," Samantha snapped. "Now are you going to untie me?"

"Yes, of course." Haley retrieved the knife and went to work on Samantha's bound wrists.

"Heavens to Betsy!" Samantha flapped her arms like a goose with broken wings in an effort to get the blood pumping through them again.

"Argh, it's like blasted red ants biting my arms!"

Haley went to the cabin, and happily found two unopened bottles of cola sitting on the opposite chair. She used the edge of the dash to open them and called for Samantha.

"Take a seat," she said as she handed one to Samantha.

They clinked bottles in salute.

"Good job, Dr. Higgins," Samantha said.

"Good job, Miss Hawke."

They spent a couple of minutes quenching their thirst and getting their energy back. Then Haley leaned against the captain's chair and started the engine. "Let's go save Mr. Boyle."

Haley's natural driving skills, along with a previous boat trip where the captain had allowed her the privilege of manning the vessel for a time, made figuring out how to drive the fishing boat relatively easy. She pulled up to Mr. Boyle just in time, it seemed. The turbulent sea had exhausted the man and he looked as if he was about to lose hold of the life ring.

Samantha reached over the edge. "Take my hand!"

Haley, having put the vessel in neutral, assisted with the rope that had so recently held her and Samantha captive. She threaded it under Boyle's armpits and together they heaved his wet and heavy body back on board. Fortunately, his energy was diminished and he didn't resist as Haley tied his hands behind his back. Before she could secure him to the rail, he turned and vomited a good amount of seawater.

"Had a bit too much to drink, huh?" Samantha quipped. She'd picked up the fishing knife and wielded it as a precaution. "He might be faking his weakness," she said.

Haley's medical instincts said otherwise, but she didn't blame Samantha for being wary.

It was a choppy ride back to the harbor, and the same twelve miles felt twice as long. Keeping her eye on the waves ahead with cursory glances behind her to make certain Boyle didn't move, Haley remained tense. Her muscles ached. Her clothing was moist and stuck uncomfortably to her body. Her hair blew loosely around her face, irritating her eyes and getting trapped between chapping lips. What she would give for a hot bath and a soft bed!

Samantha Hawke had surprised her. Her dress was torn and twisted around her body. She too, had lost her hat, but somehow, despite being windblown with goose bumps covering her arms, hair damp and stringy, and makeup running down her rosy cheeks, she looked undefeated. The frightened mouse Haley had witnessed during their taxi ride with a gun-wielding Madame Mercier had, under extreme duress, turned into a courageous lion.

When they finally reached the harbor, Haley glided the vessel to a stop. She shouted through the gathering storm. "Samantha? Are you all right to stay alone with him?"

They both stared at their captive—Haley couldn't help but think: poetic justice. He appeared awake, but docile.

Samantha flashed the knife. "I think so."

"I'll be quick." Haley managed to disembark, keeping her footing on the slick dock, and secured the boat to a pile with cold, cramped fingers.

A taxi idled on Atlantic Street, and Haley hopped in. "The nearest telephone booth, pronto!"

Haley realized she didn't have any money to pay the taxi driver or to make the call.

"I'm sorry, sir. I know this looks suspicious, but I

LEE STRAUSS

can assure you that you are assisting with police business. I'm the Boston City assistant medical examiner, and this is an emergency. I need to borrow a nickel."

The driver scowled, but after a quick assessment of Haley's physical state, grunted and handed over the coin. He shouted after her, "I ain't leavin' 'til I'm properly paid!"

When the desk sergeant at the police station answered the telephone, Haley practically shouted, "This is Dr. Higgins. Get Detective Cluney! It's urgent!"

Her voice must've effectively relayed the severity of her request as Detective Cluney was on the line far faster than any other time Haley had put in a call to him.

She explained her predicament. "You need to hurry, Detective, if you want to catch the killer."

23

*M*adame Mercier's real name was Luella Morris. Due to an unfortunate family situation, she'd found herself working for a Louisiana madam at a young age—a fact that troubled Haley, and aroused her empathy. No child should be subject to that kind of exploitation.

Though lacking a formal education, Miss Morris was sharp, and soon realized she could be a madam herself if she played her cards right. Quite literally. She learned the game of poker and won enough money to catch a bus to Boston—she'd confessed that the North had fascinated her—and rented the building on Endicott. Soon after, she donned her persona as Madame Mercier.

Miss Morris proved to be a good businesswoman, and over time, her brothel had become a financial

LEE STRAUSS

success. Unfortunately, she hadn't kept to only breaking one kind of law. Her obsession with Stefano Marchesi had been her downfall. Detective Cluney arrested her for the murders of Stefano Marchesi, Agnes O'Reilly, also known as Snowflake, and Mr. Greenfield from the raid of Edoardo Marchesi's club. Luella Morris had confessed to the killings. She'd learned about the plans for the raid that night—likely from one of her fellas, Haley thought—and packed her revolver in her purse.

Apparently, Mr. Greenfield had passed her over for the lady in the blue dress. Ballistics came back from the police lab: the casings found in the Bell in Hand and Miss O'Reilly's room were a match to Luella Morris's H&R revolver, as was the bullet Haley had plucked out of Mr. Greenfield's chest. As for Stefano Marchesi, when she told him she wanted him for herself, he'd laughed in her face, telling her she was too old for his fancy.

Bobby Ryan and James Boyle were arrested for conspiracy to commit murder and for illegal distribution of alcohol.

As for Edoardo Marchesi, Haley was in possession of a note commending her for solving the case. As she had expected, he offered her compensation. She wrote him a polite letter in response, declining, and hoped that would be the end of her connection to the Marchesi family.

Haley stared at the locked drawer of her desk, knowing what lay inside. The previous medical examiner had given it to her after a rash of morgue break-ins last winter. Times were tough, and certain folks had taken to stealing cadavers to sell on the black market.

Thankfully, Haley had never needed to use it, but after this last life-threatening experience, she wondered if she should start carrying it. The thought made her think of her dearest friend Ginger, and her feisty feminism. Ginger had no problem toting her gun around and even less problem in using it when circumstances required.

But she wasn't Ginger.

Haley left the drawer locked. She was ready to put all the unpleasantness of the previous week behind her.

SAMANTHA HAWKE HAD GOTTEN the story, the byline, and a raise. Not that her new salary even came close to what her male counterparts were making, but she felt it justified buying a new dress for work, a new tube of lipstick, and a pair of shoes for Talia. She even felt generous enough to purchase a new pair of white summer gloves for Bina.

It had only been a week since she and Haley had rescued Boyle from the ocean, tied him up to the rail, and driven the fishing boat back to shore. Talk about a reversal of fortunes!

Even though it had turned out all right—she and Haley had survived their ordeal—she'd had more than one nightmare where she had waken up soaked in a cold sweat. When she thought of what *could* have happened—.

Samantha was determined to spend more time with Talia now, taking her to the park, and reading to her at bedtime. She found she was more patient with Bina's antics and eccentricities, though she wasn't sure how long that would last.

And she had her job. The great thing about working at the *Boston Daily Record* was that something was always happening. Lots of energy and activity in the room kept Samantha preoccupied.

Johnny Milwaukee had doubted her resilience after this sensational and traumatic experience, and had created a betting pool in the office believing Samantha would back away from investigative reporting and resign herself to the safety of the ladies' pages.

Johnny didn't know her like he thought he did. She might fall, but she *always* got up again. Samantha smiled smugly to herself. Johnny was sure to be surprised when he lost that money.

THE NEXT MORNING Haley was enjoying breakfast of scrambled eggs on toast while reading the morning edition of the *Boston Daily Record*. Master Proust had found his thumb and was sucking contently as he slept in the makeshift cradle nearby. Molly had brewed a pot of coffee and brought her a cup.

"Thank you, Molly."

"You're welcome." Molly took her place at the table and joined in.

"The brothel shut down yesterday," Haley said. News reports of the case had grown fewer and slimmer over the past week, with more recent scandals and interest pieces taking their place. Madame Mercier's evil escapades were already old news, at least until her trial began.

Mr. Midnight limped into the room stopping at his food bowl for a quick bite, before jumping on Molly's lap and curling into a ball. Haley didn't like the cat in the kitchen or that Molly let the cat on her lap while she was still eating, but she knew she'd lose more than she'd gain by arguing. Instead, she turned the page to the women's section. Though she was a woman of science and academia and preferred reading material that catered to logic or serious world events, she was also a woman and found the interests in fashion, food, and family life shared by other women intriguing. Though Haley was in her forties and unmarried, it didn't mean she had to let herself become a haggard, out-of-date spinster. It was important to be able to carry on a conversation with women, and men for that matter, on topics of daily interest, even if she'd much rather discuss recent developments in forensic science.

An article just below the fold caught her eye.

WOMEN IN A MAN'S WORLD

"Oh, Molly. Listen to this." Haley cleared her throat and started reading.

"I recently met the intriguing Dr. Haley Higgins, the city of Boston's assistant medical examiner, while on a story about another apparent Mob-related shooting in the North End. Dr. Higgins, who is striking in many ways, is a thoroughly modern woman."

Molly clucked appreciatively.

Haley grinned and continued. "Though few, several female citizens in our fine city of Boston have made a name for themselves in a world dominated by men, and Dr. Haley Higgins is one of them. You might recognize her name, not from her profession, but from a recent near-tragic situation covered by this paper only a week ago.

Dr. Higgins' courage in that situation only high-lights her character."

Haley glanced up at Molly. "Oh dear. I'm starting to blush." She snapped the paper and continued to read.

"Raised on a farm, the only girl amongst three brothers, Dr. Higgins is used to holding her own with the opposite sex. That gumption took her first to Boston University and then to the London School of Medicine for Women and back again to Boston where she obtained her Ph.D. As happened to many other people, her studies were interrupted by the Great War, where Dr. Higgins served as a nurse in triage.

"Dr. Higgins has worked in her capacity as assistant medical examiner for six years, first under Dr. Angus Brown, and more recently under Dr. Peter Guthrie. The question for this writer is, will the world, and more specifically, the city of Boston, one day be ready for a female Chief Medical Examiner?"

Molly beamed at Haley. "What a splendid article. I suspect your friend Miss Hawke wrote it?"

Haley smiled at the byline. *Sam Hawke.*

"She did, indeed. One day, she'll have to feature herself."

Haley and Molly were interrupted by the doorbell, and Molly's eyes flashed with urgency. "They're here." She moved Mr. Midnight to the floor and hurried to answer the door.

Haley gently picked up the baby. "Your new mama and papa are here, little one."

When she entered the living room with the babe in her arms, Ben and Lorene Higgins stood waiting. Haley placed the baby in her sister-in-law's arms. The look of love that spread across Lorene's face was every-thing Haley had hoped for.

It was a bittersweet moment. One woman's tragedy was another woman's joy.

Ben had one arm around his wife and the other cradled under the baby. "Hey, son." His voice cracked when he said those words, and Haley's heart filled with shared emotion. If they weren't careful, they'd all break down in tears.

"He's so beautiful," Lorene said.

"Isn't he?" Molly gushed. "Just the best baby in the world."

"Thank you for taking such good care of him, Molly," Ben said. "We promise to visit you often."

"That would be so lovely." Molly was the first to pull out a handkerchief and dab the corner of her eyes.

"So, what's his name?" Haley asked.

Ben stared back before speaking. "Joseph."

"It's perfect," Haley said. For the first time since her brother's death, Haley's heart warmed at the sound of his name.

The first ring of the phone after the young family had departed caused Haley to start. It had rung inces-santly for the first few days after the story broke, but they'd enjoyed quiet today until now.

She picked up the receiver and held it tentatively along the side of her face. "Hello."

"Hello, Dr. Higgins. It's Dr. Mitchell. I haven't caught you at a bad time?"

Haley allowed her shoulders to relax. "Not at all. What can I do for you?"

"I'm hoping I can do something for you. You've had quite a trying week, and I wondered if you'd allow me to take you to dinner."

Haley felt the strange sensation of a smile spread across her face. "I'd like that."

THE MORNING COPY of the *Record* rested on Samantha's desk, folded open to her piece on Haley. Samantha liked how it had turned out and hoped that Haley would like it too. Dr. Higgins was a rather private person, so Samantha had been careful only to write what was pretty much public knowledge. With her job as a crime writer, it would be important in the future to be welcomed at the medical examiner's office, so she was very careful not to write anything that might offend.

Besides, Samantha felt that their shared, near-death experience had pushed their working relationship into something closer to friendship. At least, Samantha would like to think so.

She tapped her long painted nails on the edge of her desk. What should she do now? She was ahead of schedule for her ladies' pages—Archie August was adamant that she didn't let that flounder just because he'd given her the go-ahead to investigate without restrictions. So what should she investigate? Maybe a walk downtown would give her some ideas. She reached for her messenger bag and her camera, and was about to get up from her desk when the telephone rang.

It was a new telephone, just for her. A request Mr. August hadn't had the heart to deny her, seeing that she'd almost died while on the job.

She picked up the receiver. "*The Daily Record*, Samantha Hawke speaking."

"Miss Hawke, it's Officer Bell."

Officer Tom Bell had been checking up on her regularly since the "event", even showing up at her home on one occasion. She'd saved Tom Bell's life at the club, and now he felt he owed her.

"Officer Bell, I'm fine. You must stop—"

"It's not that. I'm not calling about your wellbeing."

"Oh. What is it then?"

"There's a body lying at the foot of the Custom House Tower. A jumper. I thought you'd like the tip."

Samantha felt ashamed of her earlier thoughts toward Officer Bell. "Thanks. I really appreciate it."

"Hey, any idea who it is?" she asked before ending the call.

"Possibly an employee," Officer Bell said. "I don't know anything more."

Samantha felt the thrill of chasing a new story bubbling up. "Thank you, Tom. I'm on my way!"

She caught the gleam in Johnny's eye as he dropped the receiver of his own telephone, and instinctively knew he'd gotten the same tip.

"Catch a ride?" Samantha asked. They'd teamed up before, why not now?

With a sly smile, Johnny shook his head. "Sorry, doll. Even though we work at the same paper, we're still competitors."

Samantha raced outside to wave down a taxi, and scowled as Johnny zoomed by in his obnoxious roadster.

Drat, that man!

THIS BOOK HAS BEEN EDITED and proofed, but typos are like little gremlins that like to sneak in when we're not looking. If you spot a typo, please report it to: **admin@laplumepress.com**

IF YOU ENJOYED READING *Death at the Tavern,* please help others enjoy it too.

- **Recommend it:** Help others find the book by recommending it to friends, readers' groups, discussion boards and by suggesting it to your local library.

- **Review it:** Please tell other readers why you liked this book by reviewing it at your vendor of purchase or Goodreads. If you do write a review, let me know at **leestraussbooks@gmail.com** so I can thank you.

Don't miss Higgins & Hawke Mysteries #2 ~ Death at the Tower.

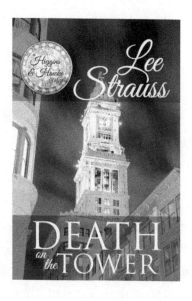

Death by Treason . . .

WHEN THE BODY of a British National is found at the base of the common house tower in Boston, assistant medical examiner, Dr. Haley Higgins has no reason to believe it wasn't suicide.

That is until Investigative Reporter Samantha Hawke gets an anonymous tip: the victim, a Mrs. Olivia Gray, was pushed from the nineteenth floor to her death.

The question is why?

Haley and Samantha work together to unravel secrets that go back to a time that no one wants to remember ∼ when shameful acts were sanctioned, and death licked at everyone's heels.

What did Mrs. Gray know, and who wanted to silence her?

On AMAZON!

Stay informed about sales and new releases by signing up for Lee Strauss' newsletter and get a FREE book!

Murder on the SS *Rosa* is where we first meet Haley Higgins. If you haven't started the Ginger Gold Mystery series, now's your chance!

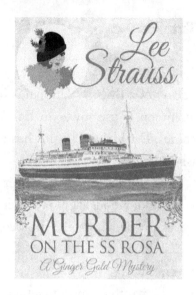

Sign up for your Free Copy
http://smarturl.it/Rosa-landingpage

Murder Aboard the Flying Scotsman

Murder by Plum Pudding

Murder on Fleet Street

A Nursery Rhyme Mystery (mystery/sci fi)

Marlow finds himself teamed up with intelligent and savvy Sage Farrell, a girl so far out of his league he feels blinded in her presence - literally - damned glasses! Together they work to find the identity of @gingerbreadman. Can they stop the killer before he strikes again?

Gingerbread Man

Life Is but a Dream

Hickory Dickory Dock

Twinkle Little Star

The Perception Trilogy (YA dystopian mystery)

Zoe Vanderveen is a GAP—a genetically altered person. She lives in the security of a walled city on prime water-front property along side other equally beautiful people with extended life spans. Her brother Liam is missing. Noah Brody, a boy on the outside, is the only one who can help ~ but can she trust him?

Perception

Volition

Contrition

Light & Love (sweet romance)

Set in the dazzling charm of Europe, follow Katja, Gabriella, Eva, Anna and Belle as they find strength, hope and love.

Sing me a Love Song

Your Love is Sweet

In Light of Us

Lying in Starlight

Playing with Matches (WW2 history/romance)

A sobering but hopeful journey about how one young Germany boy copes with the war and propaganda. Based on true events.

As Elle Lee Strauss

The Clockwise Collection (YA time travel romance)

Casey Donovan has issues: hair, height and uncontrollable trips to the 19th century! And now this ~ she's accidentally taken Nate Mackenzie, the cutest boy in the school, back in time. Awkward.

Clockwise

Clockwiser

Like Clockwork

Counter Clockwise

Clockwork Crazy

Standalones

Seaweed

Love, Tink

ABOUT THE AUTHOR

Lee Strauss is the bestselling author of the Ginger Gold Mysteries series and the Higgins & Hawke Mystery series (cozy historical mysteries), a Nursery Rhyme Mystery series (mystery, sci-fi, young adult), the Perception Trilogy (YA dystopian mystery), the Light & Love series (sweet romance) and young adult historical fiction. When she's not writing or reading, she likes to cycle, hike, and kayak. She loves to drink caffè lattes and red wines in exotic places, and eat dark chocolate anywhere.

Lee also writes younger YA fantasy as Elle Lee Strauss.

For more info on books by Lee Strauss and her social media links, visit leestraussbooks.com. To make sure you don't miss the next new release, be sure to sign up for her readers' list!

Join my Facebook readers group for fun discussions and first-to-know exclusives!

Did you know you can follow your favourite authors on Bookbub? If you subscribe to Bookbub — (and if you don't, why don't you? - They'll send you daily emails alerting you to sales and new releases on just the kind of books you like to read!) — follow me to make sure you don't miss the next Ginger Gold Mystery!

www.leestraussbooks.com
leestraussbooks@gmail.com

ACKNOWLEDGMENTS

Like the old adage, "It takes a village to raise a child," it takes a village to publish a book. With a full heart of gratitude I'd like to thank my "village."

Angelika Offenwanger - developmental editor, who reads the first dreadful drafts and helps me keep the story from falling off the rails. She's also a friend. (Thanks for your support!)

Robbie Bryant - line editor, who cleans up the first "finished" draft.

Heather Belleguelle - beta reader extraordinaire, who helps me to polish the story and complete the wordsmithing. (The day you quit is the day I quit. 😄)

Shadi Bleiken - administrator and social media guru, who helps me keep all the strings tied together and get the word out. She's a gift to La Plume Press and to the Strauss family!

Norm Strauss - partner in life and in crime. I love

how we can work and play together and never stop
finding something to laugh about.

Special thanks to my friend Dr. Anita Gaucher
who helped me with the medical scenes. (Any mistakes
in that regard are my own.)

La Plume Press

3205-415 Commonwealth Road

Kelowna, BC, Canada

V4V 2M4

www.laplumepress.com

ISBN: 9781988677910

CPSIA information can be obtained
at www.ICGtesting.com
Printed in the USA
LVHW041030141120
671371LV00005B/149

9 781988 677910